I kne   t how could I explain to Frizz that   in my life? Rees was trustworthy and dependable and everything that was good; but he wasn't exciting! Frizz wouldn't understand. Darren wasn't exciting either. He was even less exciting than Rees. He looked (I have to say it) a bit like a pudding, and he wasn't very clever; all he could really do was cook. But none of it mattered, cos Frizz was in love with him. I'd tried so hard to be in love with Rees. I wanted to be in love. I wanted the tingle factor! But it just never seemed to happen.

Girlfriends

Also by Jean Ure
in the Girlfriends series

Girls Stick Together!

Girls Are Groovy!

Pink Knickers Aren't Cool!

Boys Are OK!

Boys R Us

Boys Will Be Boys

Boys Are Back

Orchard Black Apples

Get a Life

Just Sixteen

Love is for Ever

ORCHARD BOOKS
338 Euston Road, London NW1 3BH
Orchard Books Australia
Level 17/207 Kent Street, Sydney, NSW 2000

First published in 2010 by Orchard Books

ISBN 978 1 40830 303 0

Text © Jean Ure 2010

1 3 5 7 9 10 8 6 4 2
Printed in Great Britain

Orchard Books is a division of Hachette Children's Books,
an Hachette UK company.

www.hachette.co.uk

Boys *Behaving* Badly

JEAN URE

ORCHARD BOOKS

Chapter 1

"So! What's happening at the weekend?"

It was Friday afternoon and I was wandering down the road to the bus stop with Chloe, who is my best friend at school. My best friends *out* of school are Lily and Keri and Frizz, cos we were all at juniors together. I do think it creates a special bond when you have known each other since Reception, though me and Chloe are really good mates. We met when we were sitting the entrance exam for the High School, and I was *so* relieved to see her on my first day. You need a familiar face when all your friends have gone to different places.

"Got any plans?" Chloe nudged me. "Seeing anyone?"

She was in one of her chirpy moods. She had been fizzing and bubbling all day. Normally we'd have fizzed and bubbled together, cos when Chloe's in a chirpy mood it's really catching; and usually, on a Friday, I'm feeling pretty chirpy myself. I mean, I like school and all that, but weekends are special. Today, for some reason, I was feeling like I'd stepped into a pile of sludge and couldn't get out of it.

"*Well?*" She nudged me again. "Seeing Rees?"

"Yup." I nodded.

"Doing anything exciting?"

"Not really." I stifled a sigh. "Just taking the dogs to their obedience class."

Chloe giggled. "Whatever turns you on!"

Rather crossly – since taking Bundle to an obedience class was not honestly my idea of fun – I said, "He's got to learn."

"Who? Rees?"

"No, you idiot! Bundle. He has no manners. He jumps up at people and he chases next door's cat and he won't always come when you call. He's a yob."

That's what Mrs Chesham had said: Bundle was a canine yob. "An amiable yob, I grant you. But he definitely needs to have some discipline instilled."

Mrs Chesham was the training woman; me and Bundle didn't like her. She barked all the time, and that made Bundle bark, and then he got silly and overexcited and set all the other dogs off, and everyone would be glaring at me like it was my fault. I always ended up feeling all hot and bothered.

"Poor you!" said Chloe. "What a way to spend the weekend. Glad I don't have to."

There was a pause; then she said, "*I'm* going to a party!"

She'd obviously been longing to tell me. I knew it was mean not to have asked, cos she is my very best friend at school, and it's only right to feel happy when your friends are happy. It wasn't her fault I had a dog that was a yob. I gave myself a mental thump.

"Whose party?" I said, trying to sound all bright and cheery.

"This girl that's in my reading group. Carin Saunders? One I told you about?"

I couldn't remember. I was a bit envious of Chloe and her reading group. We don't have one at my local library and hers was way too far for me to get to, so I expect the truth was I was probably crazed with jealousy.

"She's got this brother? Chad?" It all came pouring out, the words tumbling over themselves in their eagerness. Chloe's face had gone a happy pink. "He's, like, fifteen and he's going to be there, cos she says he really wants to meet me. Like normally he mightn't bother. Like if you had a party, I don't s'ppose Craig'd go, unless you were inviting someone he really, really fancied."

Was she saying this boy really fancied her? I gazed at her, doubtfully. Chloe is what my mum calls a "live wire", meaning she is always on the go, always darting here, there and everywhere, but she is not especially pretty, I don't think. She is very tiny and spidery with mad spiky hair and sticking-out teeth. Not, I hasten to add, that I am anything to boast about, being rather short and dumpy with a stupid round face like a currant bun. It's just I didn't think either of us were the sort that a boy would really, really fancy unless he got to know us and fell in love with our sparkly personalities. Hah hah!

Of course, Chloe really did have a sparkly personality; but had this boy ever actually met her? Had she ever actually met him?

The answer, in both cases, was no.

"But I've seen his photo and he's like really—" Chloe went into a mock swoon. "Gorgeous!"

"Well, hey ding a ding," I said, which is a completely stupid and meaningless thing to say, only I couldn't immediately think of anything else.

"It's all right for you," said Chloe. She looked at me, reproachfully. "You've already got a boyfriend. I'm still looking!"

I immediately felt bad. I know that boys are not the be all and end all, in other words NOT the most important thing in life, but everyone wants a boyfriend or they feel left out. And it was true that Chloe had been trying to find one for simply ages. I'd lost count of the number of boys she'd got all worked up about and then it hadn't come to anything. But she was such a bright, funny, bubbly person! She deserved to find someone.

"I do hope it works out," I said.

"Me, too," said Chloe. "Cos I fancy him like crazy!"

"And he has such a nice name," I said, encouragingly. "Chad… I really like that."

"I know." She nodded, blissfully. "I'd be on cloud nine!"

Chloe is always so open. If that had been me, I would probably have made like I didn't really care; just in case things went wrong and then people would feel sorry for me. I can't stand the thought of people feeling sorry for me! But with Chloe there isn't ever any pretence. I really admire her for that. So when we reached the High Street and prepared to part company, I said, "I'll keep my fingers crossed for you!" I honestly, genuinely meant it. I really *did* want things to work out.

"See you Monday," said Chloe. She flapped a hand. "Have fun with the dog training!"

Chloe went on her way and I settled down at the bus stop. I was starting to feel disgruntled again. Chloe would have fun: I wouldn't! Trying to make Bundle do things he didn't want to do was just, like, totally *frustrating*. Not to mention boring. For me and for poor Bundle. He didn't see the point of it, any more than I saw the point of learning equations and theorems and stuff. He might be a yob, but even Mrs Chesham had said he was an *amiable* yob. There wasn't any harm in him!

It had been Rees's idea. *Let's take the dogs to obedience classes.* Sometimes it seemed to me that everything we did was Rees's idea. But then whose fault was that? It obviously just meant that I didn't have any ideas of my own. I'd once suggested we go to the shopping centre together, but it hadn't really worked. "What do you want to *buy*?" Rees had kept asking. I hadn't wanted to buy anything! I'd just wanted to mooch around, looking. He thought it very odd. But then he'd tried to teach me to play chess, and that had been like total DISASTER. I don't have the right sort of brain for chess; I'm more like a reading-writing-type person. I think to play chess you need a brain like a computer, which is what Rees has. He is just, like, hugely logical and down to earth and full of common sense, whereas I tend to be up in the air and all over the place.

So going round the shops hadn't worked, and playing chess hadn't worked, and once we'd gone to Rees's school to watch a football match and that hadn't worked, either, not for Rees or for me. We are not terribly into sport – unlike Keri, who is never happier than when she is pounding up and down a muddy field, whacking balls about.

Thinking of it, as I waited for my bus, I decided rather glumly that the only thing me and Rees really had in common was the dogs. His dog Rufus, and my dog Bundle. We were quite happy when we were walking them round the park together. But you can't just walk round the park all the time!

Last term we'd taken them on a really *long* walk,

across the Downs. We'd both enjoyed that, until I went and got stung by a wasp and had this huge allergic reaction and practically passed out. Rees thought I was having a heart attack. He'd even given me the kiss of life! Unfortunately I hadn't been properly conscious enough to enjoy it, though probably I would just have been embarrassed. Me and Rees weren't into kissing. I did sometimes have this feeling that we ought to be, cos I mean, like, it's only natural, it's what having a boyfriend is all about. It's just somehow or other we'd never got round to it.

My bus came and I clumped up the stairs. Maybe if we did a bit more of the kissy-cuddly stuff, I thought, all the rest wouldn't matter so much. Like, where to go and what to do. It wouldn't be that important, we'd be too busy kissing and cuddling.

God! My cheeks had gone bright tomato just at the thought of it. There was obviously something wrong with me! Well, and Rees, too. Any normal boy would have got going on the kissing and cuddling ages ago. It's what boys *did*. I didn't see why I should have to take all the blame.

My phone rang; it was Frizz. She is like my best and oldest friend of all. It was always Frizz and me, Lily and Keri. The four of us had vowed to keep in touch, and we still did, though we didn't manage to get together as much as we used to. Once it had been every weekend;

now it was just occasionally. We still spoke lots on the phone, though.

Frizz was all happy and bubbling, just as Chloe had been. Full of the joys of the weekend. She asked me what I was doing and I told her about the dog training. She didn't seem to see anything odd about it.

"That sounds like fun," she said. I knew that she meant it: Frizz is never sarcastic.

I made a mumbling sound.

"You'll have the best behaved dog there ever was," said Frizz. "Maybe next time I come round he won't splat muddy paws all over me!"

I said, "I wouldn't be so sure about that... I think he's got attention deficit disorder."

"He's not the only one," giggled Frizz. "Mr Williams told me in maths today I had the attention span of a flea!"

"Oh, well, *maths*," I said. "Don't see you're likely to need much of that if you're going to be a chef."

"Except you do have to get your quantities right."

"I thought all the best chefs did it by instinct?"

"Yes." She brightened. "That's true! I can't remember the last time I followed a recipe... I always just make up my own."

I, on the other hand, would follow a recipe *slavishly*; if I ever did any cooking, that is. On the whole, I try not to. Mum asks, what am I going to do when I'm living on

14

my own? "You can't just exist on convenience foods."
I tell her grandly that I shall live on fruit and nuts and
raw vegetables. Well, and maybe a few crisps and bars
of chocolate, to vary my diet. It's important to have
a varied diet.

"Anyway," I said, remembering my duty as a friend,
"what are you doing at the weekend?" Maybe I was
half-hoping she'd say she wasn't doing anything and why
didn't we get together, but of course she was seeing
Darren. They had become like practically inseparable. Last
term they'd had a bit of a break-up, cos of Darren kissing
that totally *unspeakable* girl Darcie White, who we all
hated. But Frizz had forgiven him (which I'm not sure
I would have done) and since then they'd been closer
than ever.

"We're going up to town," gurgled Frizz, "to the Food
and Cookery Exhibition!"

I pulled a face. But I didn't say *whatever turns you on*
cos she was obviously looking forward to it, and who was
I to be all snooty? I imagined her and Darren walking
round, hand in hand, collecting samples and testing little
bits of this and that, checking out new dishes for when
they started their own restaurant, and for a moment I felt
almost sick with envy.

"On Sunday," announced Frizz, triumphantly, "we're
going to spend the day working on new recipes."

I said, "Brilliant!"

"We're making a collection...*Dawn and Darren's Cookbook.*"

I didn't quite know what to say to this. Lamely I told her that my stop was coming up and I had to go.

"Have a great weekend," said Frizz.

"And you."

I wondered what Lily was doing. She is at ballet school and is the most single-minded person I know. Her entire life revolves round her dancing. I think it must be so satisfying to have an ambition like Lily has. Something you could work towards and get obsessed with, and to simply not be bothered by all the stuff that was going on around you. I guessed that whatever Lily was doing this weekend, it would be something connected with dancing.

I was right! Just like Chloe and Frizz, she was all bubbling over with enthusiasm cos she was going to the ballet. Something I'd never heard of, danced by a woman I'd never heard of, though that is not surprising, considering how little I know about ballet.

"Who's Ana Morena?" I said. "Is she someone special?"

"*Polleee!*" Lily's voice shrieked down the phone at me. "She's famous!"

"What, like some kind of prima donna ballerina, or something?"

Lily giggled. "You don't have prima donna ballerinas! Prima donnas are opera. In ballet it's just prima ballerina."

"So is that what she is? Prima ballerina?"

"Prima ballerina *assoluta*. And we are just so lucky to have tickets! I can't believe it! We're going to wait at the stage door afterwards and see if we can get her autograph."

I said, "Who's we?"

"Me and Joel. Honestly, we're so excited!"

Joel is just like the most heavenly boy I have ever set eyes on. Being gay, he's not, strictly speaking, Lily's boyfriend, but they dance together and hang out together and love each other to bits. It's just like so romantic! Well, *I* think it is. Keri says Lily is wasting her time and ought to get herself a proper boyfriend. She is certainly pretty enough and dainty enough, she wouldn't have any trouble. She could get any boy she wanted. But she doesn't want any boy, she wants Joel, and I don't care what Keri says, I think it's really touching.

"What's Keri up to?" I said. "D'you know?"

"Haven't spoken to her. Probably going water skiing or hang gliding or jumping out of a hot air balloon."

She'd be doing something, that was for sure. Keri is always buzzing about. Her life is one round of frantic activity, and she is never, *ever* without a boyfriend. We've all given up trying to count the number she's been through!

"I'll call her," I said. "Soon as I feel strong enough."

You have to feel strong to speak to Keri. I waited till I'd got home and had tea and won a fierce battle with Craig over whose turn it was to take Bundle out. Craig is my brother and two years older than me, though most of the time he behaves like a drivelling infant – *like when it's his turn to take Bundle out.*

"I took him out yesterday!" This is what he always says, whether he did or not.

I point out that last week I took him two days running. Craig shouts that he took him on Sunday when it should have been me. I yell that I took him on Wednesday, when Craig stayed late at school. Mum then intervenes to inform us that she is sick to death of our constant fighting and why can't we behave like a normal brother and sister?

This goes on all the time. But on this occasion I win cos I'm taking Bundle to his obedience class. So Craig goes grumbling off to the park while I pick up the phone and call Keri.

"Oh, hi, Polly!" she goes. "Yah!"

I don't know why she says "yah". She is always saying it. We chat about Lily going to see the Ana Morena woman with Joel – "Time she got a *real* boyfriend!" – and about Frizz and Darren going to the cookery exhibition. Keri tells me she is spending the weekend with a girl at her boarding school who a) has her own pony and b) has a brother. The brother is also at their school. He is called Todd and he is in Year 9 and Keri has obviously set her sights on him. It strikes me that brothers (apart from mine) are quite useful, and I wonder why none of my friends have one.

"Yah! Well. How about you?" Keri.

I tell her that I'm seeing Rees; I don't mention the obedience classes.

"You don't sound very enthusiastic," she says.

I sigh. I don't mean to sigh; I'm obviously in a mood of deep self-pity.

"Dunno why you keep seeing him," says Keri. "Find someone else. I would!"

It's not that easy. It might be for someone like Keri; not for ordinary people such as myself. Besides, I wasn't really sure that I wanted to. I liked Rees! I felt comfortable with him. It was just…

"Get a bit of excitement in your life," said Keri. "You don't want to get stuck in a rut."

I wonder if this is my problem: I am stuck in a rut. Am I only going out with Rees cos it's got to be a habit? Or maybe I'm scared to break it off in case I can't find anyone else.

I spend all evening worrying about it and despising myself for being so useless. But when Rees calls to check that we're OK for tomorrow, I don't suggest we might change our plans and do something dynamic and dangerous; I just very meekly say yes.

Chapter 2

Next morning, Dad drove me and Bundle across town to meet Rees. I sat in the back with Bundle, keeping a tight hold on his lead in case he caught sight of another dog and started plunging about. Dad gets really mad when he does that. He once tore a big hole in the back seat.

"This is an excellent thing you're doing," said Dad. "Teaching that dog some manners. We should have done it ages ago."

I said that it would probably have been easier when Bundle was a puppy. "But I was only eight years old, then! I was too young. Craig should have done it."

"Your mother or I should have done it," said Dad. But Mum and Dad are busy working. Dad installs swimming pools for people and has to travel all over, and Mum is an assistant in a care home. They wouldn't have had time to go to dog training. In any case, I really couldn't see that it was necessary.

I was still in a bit of a mood. I kept thinking of Lily, going to the ballet with Joel. I pictured them sitting there together, in the romantic darkness. Would they hold hands? I wasn't sure. Frizz and Darren would! They were like practically glued together. I thought of them at the cookery exhibition, happily lost in a world of their own. I didn't think of Keri, and whatever it was that she was going to be doing. Keri lives on another planet; at least, as far as I'm concerned.

Dad dropped me off and I marched Bundle up the path and hammered with the knocker on the front door. Rees's mum opened it.

"Oh, hello, Polly," she said. "Off for some more punishment? Sooner you than me! Still, I'm sure it will be worth it in the end. Rees! Polly's here."

Rees arrived with Rufus, and together we walked up the road to the church hall, which was where the obedience classes were held. Rufus walked nicely, to heel: Bundle skittered from side to side, lifting his leg at lamp-posts then diving back across the pavement to look in someone's hedge. Rees didn't say anything, but I knew what he was thinking: *Polly has no control*. But I had! I wound the lead round my hand. "Walk properly," I told Bundle, sternly.

"I think you should say *heel*," said Rees.

"Why? He's walking OK." I said it rather crossly. I hate it when people are constantly criticising. "I don't know why we're bothering with all this," I grumbled. "Why can't we just take them up the park and let them enjoy themselves?"

"We can...afterwards."

"I'll be all hot and bothered by then."

"You shouldn't let it get to you," said Rees. "It's meant to be fun."

Huh! Some fun.

"Chloe's going to a party," I said. I don't know why I said it. I wasn't complaining; I was just *saying*.

Or maybe I *was* complaining. Some people went to parties: me and Rees went to stupid dog training. I sighed. I always seemed to be sighing, these days. It was getting to be a habit.

"We could go to a party, if you wanted," said Rees. "If you knew where there was one."

But I didn't. And I wasn't even sure how much I enjoyed parties, anyway. Meanly, I turned it on to Rees.

"You don't like parties," I said.

"I'm not terribly good at them," he agreed. "But I don't mind going, if you want."

"Well, we can't," I said, "cos I don't know where there is one. Do you know where there is one?"

He admitted that he didn't. "I could ring round, if you like."

So could I, if it came to that. I suddenly felt ashamed of myself. I was becoming nothing but a moaning misery!

I can't stand people that are always moaning. It's so negative.

"Oh, let's go and get this over and done with," I said. "Bundle, I want you to be a GOOD BOY and to PAY ATTENTION. OK?"

He gave me such a cheeky look. I should have known then that he had no intention of behaving himself. He was just about as bad as could be! When we all said "Sit", every dog in the hall obediently sat down – except Bundle. I said, "Bundle, *sit*!" and pressed like mad on his hindquarters, but he just barked and jumped up and down like he thought it was a game.

"Polly, there is no need to shout," said Mrs Chesham. "Just be firm." So then I was firm and practically squashed him flat.

"I think it's his breed," I said.

Some woman standing nearby with a poncy poodle said, "What breed?"

"Whatever he is," I said.

Mrs Chesham said that he obviously had some spaniel in him, and maybe a bit of collie.

"Both eminently trainable."

She meant that it was me, not Bundle. I was the problem!

"Just relax," she said. "Let's try again."

I prayed, inwardly. *Please, Bundle...* "SIT." Oh, and he did! I breathed a sigh of relief, and so did everyone else. Rees grinned at me, like, there you are! Nothing to it.

But then, guess what? While we're all doing our "Stay" thing, Bundle suddenly catches sight of a beautiful red, shiny ball underneath a radiator. He lunges at it and brings it to me, tail wagging in circles. Time for a game! I say, "Bundle, *drop.*" Of course, he won't. It's his ball: he found it! That is doggy logic, and if you ask me, perfectly understandable. But I can feel the atmosphere growing hostile. People are rolling their eyes and shaking their heads. That girl and her dog!

I finally manage to prise the ball out of Bundle's mouth. Unfortunately, it bounces out of my hand and lands in front of the woman and her poodle, with its stupid fancy haircut. The poodle, who up until this point has been behaving perfectly, like some kind of teacher's pet, immediately jumps on the ball. Bundle, in a frenzy of jealousy, jumps on the poodle. He wrests the ball away and takes off, joyously, round the hall, pursued by all the other dogs. It's all gone pear-shaped! *And it's all my fault.*

Mrs Chesham is not pleased. Nobody is pleased. We try doing the "Stay" thing again, but now all the dogs want to do is play. They are all over the top and won't concentrate. What I say is, there shouldn't have been a ball there in the first place. What a temptation for a poor little dog! All he wants to do is enjoy himself.

Mrs Chesham says, "Let this be a lesson...one must

have absolute control, even in emergencies. *Especially* in emergencies."

The class broke up five minutes early. I knew I wasn't popular. I heard the poodle woman complaining to someone that if a dog was going to be that disruptive, it ought to be banned.

"Wouldn't worry me," I said, as Rees and I walked up the road towards the park.

"Don't you want your certificate?" said Rees.

"What for? What good's it do? Won't get one anyway."

"You will if you work at it."

"Don't want to work at it!" I felt like telling him that Mrs Chesham was a control freak, but she's a friend of his mum so I couldn't. "Thing is," I said, "Bundle's happy!"

"Yes, but he has to learn to do what he's told, like sitting and staying and coming back when he's called."

"He does come back!"

"Only when he wants to."

We were in the park by now, with both the dogs bounding across the grass. Rees called, "Rufus! Here." Rufus immediately came. So annoying!

"You try," said Rees.

I knew Bundle wouldn't come. He was far too interested reading doggy messages.

"Bundle, come," I called. Instead of coming, he instantly took to his heels and walloped off into a flower bed. "Bundle," I pleaded, "get out of there!"

He got out, but simply went haring off towards a big pool of muddy water he likes to wallow in.

"Bundle," I cried. "Stay!"

"Gotta be firm," said Rees.

So I yelled at the top of my voice: "Bundle! STAY!" And then, in despair, "All right then, GO!"

Fortunately, we hadn't had any rain for ages and the pool had disappeared. I turned, triumphantly, to Rees. "There you are! He went when I told him."

"But he didn't *come*. And he didn't *stay*."

I was starting to get a bit prickly. "Well," I said, "and why should he? How'd you like it if some idiot was always on at you to do things you didn't want to do?"

"Rufus doesn't seem to mind."

"He's easier to train. He's younger."

"Only by a year."

"A year's a long time in dog terms. I told you Bundle was too old. I told you that right at the beginning! I don't think I'm going to go any more. Everybody hates me. I feel like *humiliated*."

"Maybe we should go at a different time? Meet different people."

"I don't want to go *at all*. Omigod! Bundle, STOP THAT!" He was rolling in something, coating himself in filth. I knew it was filth; it always was. I charged off across the grass, yelling as I went. Ugh! Yuck! Disgusting! A great pile of fresh fox poo, all wet and stinky. He'd got it all gunged up round his ears.

"Don't say a word," I said to Rees. "Just don't say a word!"

We trailed back to Rees's house, with Bundle giving off great waves of stench. I told Rees that rolling in dirt was perfectly normal dog behaviour. "It's probably a sign of great intelligence in the dog world."

Rees said in that case he was glad Rufus obviously wasn't too bright.

"I didn't say that!" I said. Though privately I do think Bundle has the superior intellect. It is another reason he cannot be trained: he is too bright. He gets bored very easily. At any rate, that is my theory.

Rees's mum came and watched as we took Bundle into the back garden and hosed him down.

"Isn't it funny," she said, "how some dogs do that?"

"Apparently it's a sign of intelligence," said Rees.

I looked at him, sharply. Was he being sarcastic? There was a definite coolness between us. It takes a lot to upset Rees, but I thought maybe I had asked for it. I knew I was being a total pain, I just couldn't seem to stop myself.

I was glad, at one o'clock, when Mrs Nicholson drove me home. I was glad that I had a genuine excuse for not staying on.

"My nan's coming over. I promised Mum I'd be back."

Rees didn't come with us, which normally he would have done. His mum obviously sensed something was wrong, cos she asked me if we'd fallen out.

"Not exactly," I said. "It's just me...I'm being a misery!"

His mum laughed and said, "Well, that's honest. What are you being a misery about?"

"Oh." I gave one of my sighs. "I've been humiliated. Bundle won't learn anything and everyone thinks it's my fault. *Rees* thinks it's my fault. I don't want to go any more!"

"Well, then, don't. You don't have to if you don't want to."

"But Rees wants to!"

"You don't have to do everything Rees wants."

But what would we do if we didn't?

"Think of something *you'd* like to do," said Rees's mum. "Don't let him bully you."

She didn't understand. Rees didn't bully me. It was just that he was the only one with any ideas...

Over lunch I told Mum and Craig about Bundle's bad behaviour. Dad wasn't back from work, so it was just the three of us.

"And then he got hold of this ball," I said, "and he wouldn't give it back, and everyone was like, *oh that awful girl and her awful dog*, and I was just like so embarrassed, and so humiliated, and—"

"*Aaaaah*," went Craig. "Poor little flower!"

"You shut up," I said. "You've no idea what it's like,

in front of all those people. *You* give it a go!"

"No way!" Craig shook his head. "Not getting me at it."

"Polly, sweetheart, if it's upsetting you that much," said Mum, "just tell Rees you don't want to do it any more."

I hiccupped. "That's what his mum said."

"Well, then, what's the problem?"

I shrugged my shoulders.

"Rees is a very understanding boy. I'm sure he wouldn't want you to do anything that makes you unhappy."

"I dunno how he puts up with her," said Craig. "Poor old Nickers!"

I glared at him. I have asked him *so many times* not to call Rees by that stupid name.

"Honestly, *girls*," said Craig. "More trouble than they're worth!"

I said, "Yeah? Well, so are boys!"

"Even Rees?" Mum studied me a moment. "You've never really forgiven him for that day in Brighton, have you?"

I squirmed uncomfortably at the memory. Me and some friends from school had gone down to Brighton for the day. There was Chloe, and our other two friends, Chantal and Katie. The idea was that we'd go with our boyfriends, so I'd gone with Rees, and Chloe had gone with a boy called Jonathan and Chantal with her boyfriend, Ben. Katie's boyfriend actually lived in

Brighton, so he'd been waiting for us at the station when we arrived. I didn't like him from the word go! He was very posh and cool, in an arrogant sort of way. What none of us realised was that he'd managed to smuggle some bottles of his dad's wine out of the house, so that while me and Chloe and the other two had gone off to look round the shops, the boys had stayed on the beach, drinking. They had all got drunk. All of them! It was horrible. Just to make matters worse, Rees had been sick on the train and *some of it had splashed on me.* Totally disgusting. But it wasn't true that I hadn't forgiven him.

"I did forgive him," I assured Mum. "He apologised, and I accepted it."

"Hmm..." Mum plainly didn't believe me. "You wait till you do something foolish and embarrassing," she said.

As a matter of fact I am always doing things which are foolish and embarrassing. I am that sort of person. But one thing I was never, ever going to do was get drunk. Not after seeing what it did to Rees. Being sick in public! *Ugh.*

I said this, very vehemently, to Mum. "I am *never* going to drink, I am *never* going to do drugs, and I am *never* going to smoke."

"So there!" said Mum.

"It's just the way I feel," I said.

Craig at this point suddenly made an unearthly hooting noise, "Whooo hoo!" and jumped up from the table. I watched in considerable irritation as he went prancing round the kitchen, flapping his arms up and down.

"What are you doing?" I said.

"Being an angel." He leaned over me, still flapping his arms. "Whooo hoo! Little Miss Goody Goody!"

Later on, when Nan was with us, Craig came into the sitting room holding something behind his back.

"Close your eyes," he said. "I've got something for you."

I said, "What?" Automatically suspicious.

"Something nice...something girly. Well, go on, close them! I'm not going to hurt you."

Frowning, I screwed my eyes shut. I felt him settle something on my head.

"There you are! Take a look."

He propelled me across to the mirror. I looked. A circle of tinfoil was sitting on my head.

Crossly I said, "What's that s'pposed to be?"

"A halo!" Craig roared triumphantly. "Cos you're just so *perfect*!"

Chapter 3

Sunday morning, Rees called to make up.

"Sorry if I was unsympathetic. Mum says you were really upset."

I thought, oh dear! Why did he have to be so *nice*? Especially when I was being so horrid.

"Wasn't your fault," I told him. "It's me, not having any control."

"Some dogs are just more difficult to train than others. But I don't think you should give up."

I said, "Why not?"

"Cos it'd make you feel like you were a failure."

"I already feel like I'm a failure. That'd just make me feel worse."

"Not if we started again, in another class."

"Why? What difference would that make?"

"It'd be easier…nobody knowing you."

He was trying really hard. I didn't mean to be

ungracious, but I couldn't help pointing out that *she* would know me.

"What, Mrs Chesham? You don't want to let her frighten you. Mum says her bark is far worse than her bite."

I said, "Huh!"

"She does a class in the afternoon. I could always see if we could go then."

I was getting all worked up again. I just *so* didn't want to go.

"It's no good," I said. "He won't learn. You can't teach an old dog new tricks."

"That's a cliché!"

I said, "So what?" I could use a cliché if I wanted. "Anyway," I said, "clichés are only clichés cos they're true."

"Not necessarily."

"Mostly." And come to think of it, he'd just used one himself, saying about Mrs Chesham's bark being worse than her bite. What cheek! Having the nerve to lecture *me*.

"Don't let's fall out again," begged Rees. "I hate it when we fall out. D'you want to go to a party next Saturday?"

Guardedly I said, "Why? Who's having one?"

"Paul Taylor's cousin."

"Who's Paul Taylor?"

"Boy in my class."

"Oh," I said, "I remember! He's that boffin person you thought might do for Frizz when she and Darren split up. Only then you decided she wasn't clever enough for him."

There was a pause.

"Yes. Well..." I could almost see him shifting uncomfortably. I wondered if he was blushing. He deserved to blush! Accusing my friend Frizz of not being clever enough. It's true she isn't any sort of genius, except when it comes to cooking, but apart from his great enormous brain, the boffin person sounded like a totally boring geek. Way not good enough for Frizz!

"Anyway," said Rees, "it's his cousin. She's having this party and she said everyone's invited."

I said, "*Everyone?* Does she live in a mansion?"

"No, I mean she told Paul to bring people. She wants lots of boys."

"Why can't she find them for herself?"

"Cos she goes to Sacred Heart. She doesn't know any."

"Oh. Right." In that case, I understood the problem; I go to an all-girls' school myself. I have to say that it is quite a comfort in lots of ways; not having to worry all the time, for instance, about whether you are impressing members of the opposite sex, but I do think it puts you at a disadvantage.

"So what d'you reckon?"

I said, "OK, let's go."

"Really?" Rees sounded relieved. "Her name's Gina, by the way. Gina Costello. She lives out near Hunters

Ford, so me and Dad'll come and pick you up. And don't worry about the dog thing. If you really don't want to go any more, that's OK."

"You can still go."

"Not without you. Wouldn't be the same."

"No, you'd be able to get on and *learn* things. I think you ought to go! I'll feel guilty if you don't."

"What's new?" said Rees. "You're always feeling guilty!"

I wondered if that was true; and if so, what did it mean? It presumably meant that I spent my life doing things that were muddled, or wrong, or just plain stupid. But I already knew that!

Monday morning I was eager to hear how Chloe had got on at her party. Had the gorgeous Chad been there? Had they hit it off? Were they going out together?

We all gathered in our favourite corner of the playing field at first break. Me and Chloe, Katie and Chantal.

"Well?" said Katie.

"Well?" said Chantal.

"Put us out of our misery!" I begged.

Chloe was guarded. Yes, Chad had been there; and yes, she thought they had hit it off, but... She didn't actually say "but". We just felt it, hanging in the air. Katie, as usual, was the first one to jump in.

"Only *thought*?" she said. "You mean you couldn't

feel it? You can usually feel it."

Chloe scrunched up her face, as if in some kind of secret anguish.

"He said he was going to ring me on Sunday."

"Next Sunday?"

"No! Yesterday."

There was a pause. I wasn't brave enough to ask the obvious question, and it seemed that neither were the other two. Not even Katie, who is known for her boldness. Chloe heaved a sigh, deep and quivering.

"I'm still waiting to hear from him."

"I'm sure you will!" Katie said it bracingly. "I mean, if he *said*..."

There was another pause. I couldn't help thinking that boys said a lot of things. Well, and girls, too, if it came to that. You couldn't always rely on what people *said*.

"Did he sound like he meant it?" wondered Chantal.

Chloe nodded, miserably. "I thought he did."

"Well, then—"

"Something probably happened," I said. "Like he suddenly got whisked off somewhere by his parents, or..."

Or what? Chloe turned, slowly and tragically, to look at me.

"Either that, or..." I floundered. I couldn't very well say, *or he just forgot*. Or even worse, *he was rushed into hospital*. Would that be worse? Well, whatever. I still couldn't say it.

"I bet he rings tonight," said Katie.

I prayed that he would. It seemed so unfair that someone as funny and sparky as Chloe should have so much difficulty finding a boyfriend. Even I had found one, and I am nowhere near as funny. And I don't really think I am sparky at all.

I told Mum about it when I got home. Me and Mum are really close; we talk about all sorts of things.

"I know boys shouldn't rule your life," I said, "but it's horrid if you feel you're the odd one out."

"You don't think," said Mum, "that maybe Chloe is trying too hard? It could be she comes across as a bit desperate. Boys are quite timid creatures! Quite easily frightened. If she could just manage to relax, perhaps things might happen."

I said, "But surely you have to do something to *make* them happen?"

"You have to create opportunities," agreed Mum. "But if people feel you're desperate they start to get uncomfortable."

She spoke as if she'd had some experience. "Were you ever desperate?" I asked.

"You'd better believe it!" laughed Mum. "At the tender age of fourteen I wrote MY LOVE LIFE R.I.P. in big black letters in my diary."

I said, "What's R.I.P.?"

"Rest in peace... It's what they put on tombstones."

"Oh! You mean you thought your love life was dead?"

"Over and done with, before it had even begun. But you see, it all came right in the end. Just as I'm sure it will for Chloe."

I wished there were some way of telling Chloe what Mum had said; I hated to see her so down. All because of some stupid boy!

I hoped so much that when I went into school on Tuesday she would be her usual sparkly self, all bubbling over because Chad had rung and they were going out together. One look at her face told me that it hadn't happened. I grumbled about it to Katie and Chantal during the lunch break, when Chloe was off having a piano lesson.

"Honestly," I said, "it is *such* bad behaviour! Promising to ring and then not bothering."

Chantal said, "Mm," and they both nodded, but they didn't seem to think it was as outrageous as I did.

"I mean, why say it in the first place? If he never meant to do it, why *say* it?"

Katie shook her head; Chantal looked blank.

"It's mean to get someone's hopes up like that!"

"I did it to someone once," said Chantal. "I didn't mean to hurt them! It was this boy I went out with a couple of times, and he was like really geeky? I just wasn't brave enough to tell him I didn't want to see him any more, so I said I'd ring him, only I didn't, and it was awful cos he kept ringing me, and I kept begging Mum to say I was out, and it got like really embarrassing?"

"What happened?" said Katie.

"Well, he stopped in the end. Thank goodness!"

"It was still a horrid thing to do," I said.

"I know," said Chantal, "I know! I felt dreadful. But it's really difficult. *You* try telling someone you don't want to see them any more!"

"Way I do it," said Katie, "I just keep like making excuses? Like I've got to go and visit my nan, or I've got loads of homework to get through, or I've got a cold, or something. They have to be really thick not to get the message."

"But this Chad person wasn't *going* out with Chloe," I said. "So what's the point of saying he'd ring her if he didn't mean it?"

"Well…" Katie shrugged. "I guess sometimes people say what they reckon you want to hear."

I had to admit that made a sort of sense. It didn't *excuse* it; but I could see you might mistakenly think you were making someone happy. I told Katie and Chantal what Mum had said, about how maybe Chloe came across as too desperate. I felt a bit disloyal, saying it behind her back, but it wasn't gossiping. I really wanted to help.

"Thing is," said Chantal, "even if it's true, how do we tell her?"

"We don't," said Katie. "Not unless…"

They both turned to look at me. Although we are all friends, I am the one who is closest to Chloe.

"No!" I heard my voice wailing, pathetically. "I couldn't! I wouldn't know what to say!"

They didn't press me. "Maybe she'll hear from him tonight," said Chantal.

But of course she didn't. I think we all accepted, now, that it wasn't going to happen.

"I think you ought to ask this girl in your reading group," I said. "The one that gave the party. After all, she's his sister. I think you should ask her why he hasn't rung."

"You have to be joking!" said Chloe.

"I'm not, I'm serious. I think you have a right to know."

"Bad idea," said Katie. "Very bad idea. It'd make her look…ahem!" She cleared her throat. "Desperate."

"Yes, and you desperately don't want to look desperate!" That was Chantal, weighing in. Chloe gave a loud screech of laughter. It sounded a bit mad to me.

"Who says anything about desperate?" She raked her fingers through her hair, making it all stand on end. "Do I look desperate?"

Katie giggled. "No, just bonkers!"

"This is it," said Chloe. "I've gone stark staring bonkers!"

I was glad her sense of humour had come back, but I was still cross at the way she had been treated.

I said, "Know what I think?"

"No, what?" said Katie.

"I think life'd be a whole lot simpler if we didn't have to bother about boys."

There was a silence.

"Come again?" said Chantal.

"I think it'd be so much easier if we didn't have to bother with them... Like not until we were, say, twenty-one or something. And the same for them! They wouldn't have to bother with us. Then all of a sudden it'd be like a switch was turned on, and you'd start taking notice."

"Why wait till twenty-one?" said Katie. "What's the point of that?"

"Cos I think they'd be easier to cope with. It would save all this—" I waved a hand "—all this constant worry!" Like what to wear, and what to say, and what to do. How far you ought to go. How far other people went. Were you lagging behind? Were you *normal*?

Katie and Chantal were both critically studying me, like I was some sort of specimen in a jar.

"Some of us," said Katie, "don't *have* constant worry. Some of us just get on and enjoy life!"

"Polly, you are *so* funny at times," said Chantal.

I knew they thought I was seriously weird. But it's all

very well for them! Katie is one of those people that positively oozes confidence from every pore. As for Chantal, she is just about *the* most beautiful person I know. She has skin like brown velvet and looks like a model. What do either of them have to worry about?

Chloe confessed to me later, as we walked up the road together at the end of school, that she thought I might be right. She meant about boys.

"Sometimes I just get like worn out. You know?"

I did know. I knew exactly! It is such a comfort to have someone like Chloe to talk to. Someone *not* beautiful and *not* madly confident. Just ordinary, like me.

"All this bother about how you're going to meet them, and what they're going to think of you, not to mention squeezing *spots*." She had this great big one, on her chin. I felt for her. "And all this rushing round to parties, hoping *this'll* be the one. Only it never is," she ended, glumly.

"I'm going to a party," I said.

The minute the words were out of my mouth, I wished I could take them back. Why do I do these things??? I knew how fragile Chloe was feeling. I honestly hadn't meant to boast! It just slipped out.

"I don't s'ppose it'll be worth going to," I said. "It's this boy in Rees's class. He's a real geek!" Not that I had ever met him. He just sounded like a geek. "I'm only going cos Rees wants to. I don't really like parties."

42

"I do," said Chloe. "Usually!" And then to my horror she burst into tears. "I wish I believed in God," she said. "Then I could go and be a nun!"

I immediately told her about Mum and her tombstone. "MY LOVE LIFE R.I.P.. She thought it was all over, and she was only fourteen!"

"Well, I'm almost thirteen and mine hasn't even begun," wailed Chloe.

"Neither's mine," I said, "if it comes to that."

"You've got Rees! He gave you the kiss of life!"

"Yes, but I was unconscious. And he hasn't done it since." I then confided to Chloe what I wouldn't have confided to another living soul, except Frizz. Well, and maybe Lily. "We don't really have what you'd call a love life."

"You mean—" Chloe wiped her nose on the back of her sleeve. She looked at me, hopefully. "You mean, he doesn't..." She waved a hand. "He doesn't kiss you?"

I blushed. "Not really. We sometimes hold hands. But mostly we just, like...talk?"

She cheered up considerably when she heard that, so that I went on my way feeling I had done something noble. It is not easy to admit that your love life is non-existent. Not even to a best friend. I certainly would never had admitted it to Keri, who rang me after tea to tell me that she had just met this really cool guy. He went to some posh boys' school in Hastings, near to her posh

43

boarding school, and he was called Dermot.

"Cool," she said, "or what?"

I thought, not especially. And why tell *me*? She was always meeting boys. It wasn't news any more.

"We need somewhere to go," said Keri. "Know where there's anything happening?"

Proudly I said that *I* was going to a party.

"Oh, good! We'll come along. Where is it?"

Keri is just, like, *un-be-lievable*. I protested rather feebly that you can't go round inviting yourself to other people's parties. She said, "Why not? The more the merrier! What's the address?"

I told her that I didn't know the address. "It's out Hunter's Ford somewhere, so you wouldn't be able to get there anyway. Well, *he* wouldn't. Not if he lives in Hastings."

Breezily, Keri said that he didn't *live* there. He just went to school there. "He's a weekly boarder, like me. Find out the address and let me know."

I wasn't sure that I wanted to. I said, "I wouldn't bother, honestly. It doesn't sound like it's going to be a very *good* party."

"Why not? Who's giving it?"

"I don't know, some girl called Gina something…Gina Costello? She's the c—"

"Oh, I know Gina! Her mum owns the salon where my mum gets her hair done. That's OK! I'll give her a call.

44

Hey, this'll be fun!" said Keri. "Long time since we've been at a party together."

I rang off, thinking to myself that if Katie oozed confidence, Keri was positively *pushy*. But I did sort of envy her…

Chapter 4

By the time Saturday arrived, I found that I'd managed to talk myself into a state of excitement and was really looking forward to the party. It would be fun! When I was younger I used to be all silly and shy and self-conscious. I hated going to parties in case I ended up standing in the corner by myself, or crying in the bathroom.

I still wasn't sure that I'd be brave enough to go on my own, but so long as I was with Rees, I felt safe. I knew he wouldn't desert me to go rushing off after some other girl, cos Rees wasn't like that. He was dependable. Also, of course, it meant that I would have something to tell the others on Monday. Katie and Chantal weren't the only ones to have a social life!

The big decision, as always, was what to wear. If anyone can get it wrong, it's me! If I went in jeans, everyone else would be dressed up; whereas if I dressed up, you could just bet that everyone would be in jeans.

I did that, once. I was going to this party that I thought was going to be really posh, so I did myself up like a Christmas tree, all strung about with beads and bangles and my *best* sparkly top. But when I got there I found everybody dressed in rags and tatters, like T-shirts torn practically to shreds and jeans hacked off at the knee with bits all trailing. One girl even had holes where her bum cheeks were, so that her knickers showed through! It turned out it was a grunge party and no one had told me! That was one of the times I went and cried in the bathroom. Well, I didn't actually cry; just sat for ages on the edge of the bath wishing Dad would come and pick me up and take me home.

I decided on this occasion, as Keri was going to be there, I would *half* dress up. Keri isn't into grunge. She is our style guru and always looks like a trillion dollars. And she always gets it right! If she was the only one dressed up, then everyone else would just look pathetic.

So I put on my favourite top, which is pink, and so what? Craig says it's girly, but I *am* a girl. I see nothing wrong in it. To go with the top, I wore my second favourite skirt, which is like a sort of kilt, but rather short. Well, very short, as a matter of fact. But I wore a pair of thick ribbed tights underneath, so it wasn't like indecent or anything. It still didn't stop Craig going, "Ooh! Sexy!" as I went downstairs.

Well, that is *exactly* the sort of remark guaranteed to

get Dad all worked up. Sure enough, he spun round at once, eyes narrowed.

"That skirt's a bit short, isn't it?" He appealed to Mum. "It is, isn't it? Far too short! She can't go out like that."

Behind his back, Craig was pulling faces and mouthing at me: "*Far too short... Can't go out like that!*" Fortunately, Mum came to my rescue. She told Dad not to be such an old fuddy-duddy.

"There's absolutely nothing wrong with it! She looks very pretty."

"Sexy," said Craig.

Honestly, there are times I feel like bashing him. Dad had gone all red and apoplectic.

"Why does it have to be so short? She wouldn't be allowed to wear it to school – and that's all girls!"

"Yeah, gonna be *boys* around tonight," said Craig.

"Exactly my point," said Dad.

"For goodness' sake!" Mum sounded exasperated. "She's going to a party! What do you expect?" I love it when Mum is on my side; she can always talk Dad round. "We went to parties ourselves once...or have you forgotten?

Dad muttered, "It was different, then."

"That's right," said Mum. "We were young, now we're old. Don't tell me you've forgotten that party where we met and what I was wearing!"

Dad looked shifty. Craig immediately pounced.

"What?" he said. "What were you wearing?"

"Well, put it this way," said Mum. "It wasn't a boiler suit."

"What was it?"

"Just let's say there wasn't a great deal of it. Your dad didn't seem to object then. Leave the poor girl alone, both of you! Take no notice of them, Polly."

It was easier said than done, with Dad still glowering and Craig grinning like an idiot and mouthing *"Sexy"* behind Dad's back. I almost felt like rushing back upstairs and pulling on a pair of jeans. Mum squeezed my arm.

"I'm sure Rees will be very proud to be seen with you."

"Anyway, it's OK." Craig turned to Dad, man to man. "I'll be there to keep an eye on her."

CRAIG was going to be there? "Who invited you?"

"Old Brainiac."

I presumed he meant Paul Taylor. "So who are you taking?"

"Not taking anyone. Pick someone up when I get there."

"I beg your pardon?" said Mum.

"Pick someone up when I get there."

"Pick someone up?"

"I mean, meet someone," said Craig. "Meet someone there."

Even Craig has this huge confidence in himself. I really don't know why, since he isn't anything special.

Well, I don't think he is. Girls do seem to go for him, though.

"He's hoping to *pick someone up*," I told Rees, as his dad drove us out to Hunter's Ford.

"Meet someone!" roared Craig.

I sniffed. "You'll be lucky."

"He might be," said Rees. "According to Paul, there's going to be simply loads of girls there. She's invited practically the whole of her class."

I wondered how an entire class, plus any boys they might bring with them, plus me and Rees, and Keri and Dermot, and Craig and the Brain, were all going to fit in. I was thinking of our front room at home. Last time I'd had a party I'd invited twelve people, and *that* had been a crowd. Craig said scornfully that people didn't have parties in their front rooms any more.

"They hire a hall. Either that or go to a bowling alley, or something. That's what I'm going to do next time. Go bowling!"

I said, "I thought that was an old people's thing... playing bowls."

"Not *bowls*, you idiot! *Bowling.*"

"Ten-pin bowling," said Rees. "We could try going some time, if you wanted."

"What, with her?" said Craig. "You gotta be joking! She couldn't hit a ten-ton truck."

It wasn't any use me saying I could, because I probably couldn't. Silently, Rees stretched out a hand and took mine. He squeezed it and grinned at me. I was a bit wary in case Craig happened to notice, in which case he'd be bound to make some kind of stupid and embarrassing remark; but at the same time it gave me a nice cosy glow of comfort.

The hall where the party was held was really big; almost as big as our gym at school. I could understand, now, why Gina had been so eager for loads of people to come. Even with the whole of her class plus all the rest of us, there were still wide stretches of open space.

All down one side there were tables laid out with food and drink. Craig said, "Way to go!" and headed straight for it. He has absolutely *no* sense of shame. By the time me and Rees caught up with him he was already stuffing himself with sausage rolls.

"Pity about the booze," he said.

"Why?" One whole table was crammed to bursting with cans of Coke and fizzy drinks and fruit juice. "What's wrong with it?"

"No hard stuff." Craig snatched another sausage roll and went busying off into the throng.

"What's he talking about?" I said. "*Hard* stuff?"

"I think he means, like, spirits? Whisky, and gin, and stuff?"

"That's alcohol," I said. "He's not allowed to drink alcohol. Just showing off, as usual."

"He likes to get you going," said Rees. "There's Paul! Come and say hello."

I allowed myself, rather reluctantly, to be dragged down the hall to where the great Paul Taylor stood, lordly surveying the scene. So this is the huge mega-brain, I thought. The one that was too good for my friend Frizz. Well, huh! He wasn't much to look at. Frizz mightn't be what you'd call pretty, but at least she's not all puddingy. And she doesn't have a pasty face! I knew I was being *body-ist*, which I usually try very hard not to be, but I was still quite upset on Frizz's behalf.

Rees introduced us, and we both said "Hi". Then the Brain said, "So you're Polly?" in a distinctly superior sort of way, and I said, "So you're the Brain," meaning to be sarcastic but he took it seriously and smiled and looked smug. After that, we ran out of conversation.

"He's no great talker," said Rees, as we moved away.

I said, "No, cos I suppose we're all too stupid for him."

"I think he's a bit shy, actually. He's never had a girlfriend. Girls don't really seem to get turned on by him."

I said that I could see why they wouldn't.

"Why?"

"Well! I mean…he's not exactly swoon material."

I thought that was rather good: *swoon material*. I expected Rees to laugh, but he didn't.

"Know what?" he said. "You'd be at my throat if

I made that sort of remark about a girl."

I squirmed a bit at that, cos I knew that he was right.

"It's not just physical," I muttered. "It's his personality."

"You reckon?"

"Yes! I do." Even though Frizz isn't pretty, she is very sweet and generous. Unlike the Brain, who was just cold and aloof. I tried explaining this to Rees, but he shook his head.

"He's not cold and aloof, he's just self-conscious. You probably think it's easy for boys, but we're every bit as sensitive as you about the way we look – and *we* can't do as much about it. You can mess around with your hair and make-up. We can't."

Of course I felt bad, then, harbouring all those venomous thoughts. It was Rees I ought to be cross with, not the Brain. *He* wasn't the one that reckoned Frizz was beneath him. He'd never even met her! Still, I didn't want to quarrel. Not at a party. Not at any time, really.

"Let's go and talk to Keri," I said. I'd just seen her breeze in with her new boyfriend, the gorgeous Dermot. He *was* actually quite gorgeous. He had luscious thick black hair, very wavy without being curly (I hate curls!) and bright blue eyes that twinkled and flashed. Yuck! That sounds really gooey. But it happened to be true. Keri really did know how to pick them! She just couldn't keep them, that was the problem.

As always in such situations, I was instantly struck

53

dumb and couldn't think of a single intelligent thing to say. Or even an unintelligent one, come to that. I just stood there, beaming, like some kind of garden gnome, and all the time I was thinking how glad I was that I had chosen to wear my favourite top and my second-favourite skirt. I would have been mortified if I'd come in a pair of ratty old jeans!

"Great party," said Keri. "Dunno why you thought it wouldn't be any good! I'm going to have my next one in a hall. It's going to be huge! Even huger than this. Have you seen Gina's mum and dad? They're hiding in one of the side rooms! But they've hired these bodyguards... See, over there?" She pointed across the hall, to where two bigger boys were standing. "That one's Charlie, the other one's Dave." She giggled. "They're here to keep us in order! Make sure no one does anything they shouldn't, like *inappropriate behaviour* or smuggling drugs."

Alarmed, I said, "Drugs?"

"Oh, there's always someone!"

"Some idiot," said Rees.

"Yeah, right."

Keri didn't sound specially bothered. I couldn't help thinking that she was growing up far faster than the rest of us. I am *so* unsophisticated! I didn't know anything about drugs. Not that I really wanted to, but did it mean I was young for my age? I was pretty sure Frizz and Lily were the same. And maybe Chloe. Maybe Chantal. I wasn't so sure about Katie. I asked Rees if he knew anything, and he said, "As much as I need to."

"What's that mean?"

"Means I don't want anything to do with them!"

"Me neither," I said.

"So what's the problem? You've got your worried look."

"It's just that sometimes," I said, "I think I'm too innocent... Seriously! I do. I live in a state of complete ignorance. When it comes to drugs I don't know the first thing."

"Shouldn't let it bother you," said Rees. "There are some things that aren't worth knowing. They happen to be one of 'em."

I suppressed a sigh. "You are always so *sensible*," I said.

"You mean boring," said Rees.

"I don't! I mean sensible."

"Yeah, well...I reckon one of us has to be. Incidentally, next Saturday we're going to Hadleigh House. D'you want to come?"

I immediately said, "Yes!" Not wanting to miss out. And then, more cautiously, "What is it, exactly?"

"It's like this historic house you can go round? They've got this old car museum." Rees's eyes gleamed as he told me about it. "They've got Daimlers and Lanchesters and really old stuff from like way back. That's what me and Dad want to see!"

I recoiled slightly. *Old cars?* I wasn't interested in looking at old cars!

"Honestly," said Rees, "you'd love them! They're your sort of thing. Like sort of...*toy* cars. You know? Like in the London to Brighton rally. You've seen the London to Brighton rally?"

I said, "Mm." Guardedly. I'd once stood at the side of the road for hours with Dad and Craig, watching these ancient old vehicles go trundling past. It had been fun for about ten minutes, cos some of them were like really cute and quaint, like dolls' prams on wheels, but it had got a bit boring in the end. I wasn't really sure that I wanted to go and look at a whole load of them just lined up in a museum.

"They let you go and sit in them, if you're lucky! Sometimes they even take you for a drive." He obviously sensed that he wasn't exactly filling me with enthusiasm. Quickly he said, "There's loads of other things. It's not just cars. Mum wants to see the house and gardens."

"I s'ppose they don't have any animals?" I said, hopefully.

"You mean, like a private zoo or something?"

"No!" I howled it at him. I don't approve of zoos. "I meant like horses, or...pet lambs, or something. Pet lambs they don't *eat*. I don't suppose they have any of those?"

"I don't think so." Rees sounded doubtful. "They've got peacocks! And this big park, with deer."

"Deer?" I perked up when he said that. I adore deer!

"So d'you feel like coming?"

"I'll have to check with Mum first," I said, "in case she's already arranged something. But if she hasn't—"

"Let me know."

"OK." My gaze strayed across the room. "Omigod," I said. "Look at Keri!"

She and Dermot were like glued together.

"Inappropriate behaviour," said Rees, solemnly.

I giggled. "Trust Keri!"

Even as we watched, one of the bodyguards – Charlie, I think it was – went over and gently tapped Dermot on the shoulder. I saw him shaking his head and wagging a finger in mock reproof. I reflected that if I ever had a big party in a hall, poor Dad would never be able to relax. He would be in and out every five seconds, terrified about what might be going on. While Mum worries about Craig, and whether he is treating girls with the proper respect, Dad worries about me, and whether my skirts are too short. He would go ballistic if he saw me in a clinch with a boy! Not that it seemed very likely; not, at any rate, with me and Rees. Not with me and anyone, except in my dreams. When it came to real life, it just didn't happen. I would probably only be embarrassed, anyway.

*

Keri rang me next day. "That was a really good party," she said. "Dermot really enjoyed it."

I said, "Yes, I saw!"

"What, poor old Charlie coming on all heavy?" Keri gave one of her great swooping shrieks of laughter. "All we were doing was indulging in a bit of slurpy lurv… Hey, listen! Reason I'm ringing… What are you doing next Saturday?"

Playing for time, I said, "Dunno yet. Why?" I couldn't help feeling tempted. I knew I oughtn't to be, when I was supposed to be going out with Rees; but on the other hand I hadn't actually made any firm arrangements with him. I'd said I'd have to ask my mum.

"I need you to make up a foursome," said Keri. "Dermot's got this friend who'd like to meet you? Rory?"

Rory. A neat name! I liked the sound of it. But why me? I said this to Keri and she said, "Why not you? Dermot saw you at the party, right? He thought you looked cute."

I said, "Really?"

"Really!"

It was hard not to feel flattered, but I wasn't going to give way immediately. If at all. I said, "Huh." And then, "Hm!" I wanted her to know that I didn't necessarily believe all that she told me. Though naturally I would have liked to.

"So is it OK?" said Keri. "Can I say you'll come?"

"Mm… Maybe. I'll think about it." I didn't altogether trust Keri; not when it came to boys. "What's he like?"

"Rory? He's OK!"

"He's not, like, peculiar looking?"

"Of course he's not peculiar looking! Dermot doesn't have friends that are peculiar looking." And, in any case, looks are not supposed to matter. "Oh, come on, Pol! Don't play hard-to-get. I need you!"

I wondered what she needed me for, and why she was asking me instead of Lily. Lily, after all, was her best friend.

"*Please*, Polly! Pretty please! We're going to go boating in Rutger's Park, then we're going for a pizza, then back to my place. *Please*, Polly, say you'll come!"

Weakly I said, "But what about Rees?"

"Tell him you have other plans! It's not like you and he are really getting anywhere," said Keri.

And who wanted to go and look at old cars, anyway?

I made one last attempt at controlling myself. "Why not ask Lily?" I said.

"I did, she can't make it. Anyway, she's still mooning about over Joel. In any case, I told you, Dermot reckons you and Rory'd get on."

And he'd thought I was cute…

"OK," I said. "I'll come!"

Chapter 5

I don't usually tell lies. Not that I'm a specially good sort of person; I just think how *I* would feel if somebody told me one. If I knew about it, that is. Like, *I can't see you this weekend cos I'm going somewhere with my mum and dad.* And then you discovered they were seeing someone else. That would be really hurtful. It was why I didn't want Rees ever to find out. I desperately didn't want him to be hurt!

So why do it, then? That is what I kept asking myself. *Why am I doing this?* It's what Frizz asked me, when I rang her up begging for help.

"If ever you bump into Mum, like if she comes into your dad's shop or anything, or if you come round to my place and she asks you, which she won't, cos there isn't any reason why she should, but just in case...d'you think you could say I was with you all afternoon?"

"Which afternoon?" said Frizz.

"Well, like…tomorrow?"

"*Saturday*? I'm seeing Darren."

"That's all right, Mum wouldn't know! You could still say I was with you."

"But why?" said Frizz.

Questions, questions! Why do people have to keep asking *questions* all the time? Why can't they just do what you want? Frizz was supposed to be my best friend!

"Where are you *really* going to be?"

I muttered, "Making up a foursome with Keri."

"What, you and Rees, and—"

"Not Rees."

There was a pause.

"So who?" said Frizz. She was suddenly sounding all suspicious and accusing. I took the phone away from my ear. I was dripping sweat; a sure sign of guilt! "Who are you going with?"

"Me and Keri and her boyfriend and…her boyfriend's best mate."

"You mean you're going on a blind date?"

"Yes! Well… N–no. Not exactly. I mean…I know Keri's boyfriend. Dermot."

"But you don't know his mate!"

I had to admit that I didn't.

"And you want me to lie to your mum?"

"Only if she asks. Which she won't!"

"So why—"

"I just don't want it getting back to Rees!" I had thought of making the excuse that we were visiting my nan, or even ringing up Saturday morning and saying I didn't feel well. But Craig would know it wasn't true and he was in the same class as Rees, and it wasn't an atom of use asking him not to tell. They say girls can't keep secrets, but neither can some boys. The only solution was to pretend I was with Frizz.

"Just do it for me?" I pleaded. "*Please!* Just this once."

"I don't approve," said Frizz.

I felt like telling her not to be so self-righteous, but I guess, in my heart, I didn't approve either.

"Why are you *doing* it?"

"Cos Keri asked me."

"Why couldn't she ask one of her posh friends? Why couldn't she ask *Lily*?"

"Lily's too taken up with Joel."

"But he's not her boyfriend. Rees is your *boyfriend!* What are you going to tell him?"

"Going to tell him I'd forgotten I was s'pposed to be spending the day with you."

"*What?*"

I said it again, a bit louder. "Going to tell him I'm spending the day with you!"

"That's mean," said Frizz.

I knew it was mean. It was utterly despicable. But how

could I explain to Frizz that I longed for a bit of romance in my life? Rees was trustworthy and dependable and everything that was good; but he wasn't exciting! Frizz wouldn't understand. Darren wasn't exciting, either. He was even less exciting than Rees. He looked (I have to say it) a bit like a pudding, and he wasn't very clever; all he could really do was cook. But none of it mattered, cos Frizz was in love with him! I'd tried so hard to be in love with Rees. I *wanted* to be in love. I wanted the tingle factor! But it just never seemed to happen. I muttered something about being too young to be tied to one person.

"So if you don't want to go out with him any more, just *tell* him," said Frizz.

I knew that I wasn't brave enough. Apart from anything else – like not wanting to hurt him – there was this little pinprick of doubt at the back of my mind. Suppose things didn't work out between me and Rory...then where would I be? If I'd broken with Rees?

"It's not right," said Frizz. "Creeping around behind his back."

I never thought the day would come when Frizz would start lecturing me. Frizz of all people! I did my best to work up a bit of indignation.

"Pardon *me*," I said. "All is fair in love and war."

Rees would have told me that was a cliché. Frizz just made an impatient scoffing noise.

"Know what?" she said. "I bet Keri only asked you instead of Lily cos she didn't want any competition."

What cheek! What a thing to say! Now I really was indignant. *Of course* I know that Lily is far prettier than I am, she is the prettiest of all of us, but the reason Keri had asked me was cos Dermot thought I looked cute. Only I couldn't very well say that to Frizz.

"As a matter of fact," I said, coldly, "the reason she asked me was because we were all at this party on Saturday and Dermot thought I'd get on with his friend."

"Really?" said Frizz.

I said, "Yes! Really."

Long silence.

"So will you do it for me?" I whispered. "*Please?*"

"I'll do it for you this time," said Frizz. "But I'm not going to do it again!"

I am such a coward. I still wasn't brave enough to ring Rees and tell him; I texted him, instead.

Sorry sorry sorry! Can't C U 2morrow after all. 4got I promised Frizz I'd spend the day with her. Really sorry!

I nearly didn't pick up when my phone rang and I saw that it was Rees. I sort of half-hoped, in a way, that he'd be mad at me, cos then I could have got on my high horse and reminded him that Frizz was my best and oldest friend and that I couldn't possibly let her down. But Rees isn't a person that gets mad. He was nice as could be! He said what a pity it was cos he thought I would really have enjoying going round Hadleigh House.

"I asked Mum and Dad if we could make it next week, instead, but they can't manage it next week."

"Maybe the week after?" I said.

"It won't be open then. It's only open a few weeks a year."

I said, "Ah." Thinking, how pointless was *that*? A few weeks a year? Hardly worth opening at all. "Maybe next year," I said, lamely.

"Yeah. Maybe. Where are you going with Frizz?"

"Oh…you know! Just round and about. We haven't properly decided yet."

"You don't think *she'd* like to come?"

That threw me into a total panic. "Well, no, I mean, she'll probably want to go to some cookery thing, some exhibition or something. You know what she's like!"

"Well, have fun," said Rees.

"And you."

Needless to say, him being so nice made me feel absolutely terrible – which I knew I deserved to. It is horrid, feeling ashamed of yourself. I almost rang Keri to tell her I'd changed my mind. I did actually dial her number, but then ever-so-quickly cut myself off before the phone could start ringing. I guess I wasn't quite as ashamed as I ought to have been.

Anyway! Whatever. I got my comeuppance, as Nan would say. I woke next morning to feel these hideous griping pains in my stomach. I knew at once what it was. By the time I'd crawled out of bed and crept downstairs, my insides were all churning about like a cement mixer. Mum pushed a bowl of cornflakes at me, but I had to tell her I wasn't hungry.

"She's on a diet," said Craig.

I said, "I am not!"

"I hope you're not," said Mum.

"I'm not!"

"Ought to be." Craig puffed out his cheeks and made a big stomach-shape in the air with his hands.

"Craig, don't do that," said Mum. "There's absolutely nothing wrong with your weight, Polly. But you've got to eat something! If you don't want cereal, have some fruit. Have a banana or an apple."

To stop her getting fussed I forced myself to chomp on a banana, but it all clogged up in my mouth and made me feel sick. In the end, I had to ring Keri whether I liked it or not.

"I can't come!" I wailed.

Keri said, "What d'you mean, you can't come?"

"This afternoon...I can't come!"

"Why not?"

"I've got my period."

"So?"

"I feel awful!"

Keri made an impatient clicking noise with her tongue.

"I've told you before, it's all in the mind."

Rather snappishly, I said, "It's not in the mind, it's in my tummy! There's a big hand, squeezing and twisting and—"

"Spare me the details!" said Keri. "You don't get enough exercise, that's your problem."

"Pardon me," I said, "I take Bundle out *regularly*."

"Yes, but you don't do enough PE. The least little thing and you wriggle out of it."

Honestly, I do find these mad sports fanatics rather tiresome. Once at school, when I begged Miss Southgate to let me off hockey as I had a really bad stomachache, she accused me of "Just making excuses". But she told me to take myself off to the sick-room and I lay there the whole afternoon rolling about in complete agony. While I was rolling, Miss Southgate looked in and said, "You know, if you'd joined the rest of us on the hockey field, you'd have run that out of yourself!" Just, like, *totally* unfeeling. Like Keri.

"Oh, come on, Polly!" she said. "Don't be such a wimp. You can't let me down at this stage! Just go and take some paracetamol, or something."

"They don't work!"

"I'll tell you what works," said Keri. "*Forgetting about it.* That's what works! I remember one time I had this ghastly toothache? Like someone sticking a needle into me? And I had to go and play in a tennis tournament, and guess what?"

"You won." She always won.

"Yes, but more than that!"

"Your tooth fell out." I said it in these rather sour tones, cos I just get so tired of Keri preaching at me all the time.

"No, you idiot!" She gave one of her shrill cackles of laughter. "The pain went away and never came back. See? This is what I mean: mind-over-matter. I shall expect you at three o'clock. *Don't let me down!*"

I don't know what it is about Keri, she always manages to get her own way. Well, with me she does. I don't stand up to her enough! The others do; even Frizz. When we were at Juniors, Frizz used to be a bit scared of Keri, but these days she sticks up for herself. She doesn't let anyone push her around. And Lily just gets on and does her own thing, regardless. Lily can be quite stubborn, in her own quiet way. I just let myself be walked all over!

When it was time to go, Mum said if I just hung on for five minutes she'd give me a lift. I really would have liked one, cos it's a whole long bus journey to Keri's then a LONG walk up this *really* steep hill, but Mum thought I was going to see Frizz, and Frizz lives in absolutely and utterly the wrong direction. For one wild moment I thought of saying we were actually meeting at Keri's, only I couldn't quite rouse the energy to tell yet more lies. So I said it was OK, I'd make my own way, and set off with gritted teeth for the bus stop. The cement mixer was still churning inside me, and I was sure I could feel a spot breaking out on my chin. I kept fingering it, and prodding, until I just knew it had to be glowing red like a tomato.

I thought, *this is all your own fault.* If I'd been going to Hadleigh House with Rees, I could have rung and said I wasn't well, and Rees would have been sympathetic and said he hoped I'd soon feel better. *He* wouldn't have bullied me.

Thinking about Rees didn't help any. It just made me feel sorry for myself. Guilty, too, of course; but mainly just sorry.

I trudged at snail's pace up the hill. An old lady overtook me, going like the wind; I wondered how she managed it. I was hoping that when I got to Keri's I'd be able to sit down for a minute, but even before I'd gone up the path the front door was thrown open and Keri came bursting out, followed by Dermot and another boy.

"Polly, *there* you are! Where have you been? I said three o'clock! This is Rory, by the way... Rory, this is my friend Polly."

Rory said, "Hi, Polly." I just said hi. Omigod, he was dreamy! Definitely *not* the boring drippy geek I'd secretly been expecting. He had eyes that were ice cold blue, and blond hair which was almost white, and this deep, dark, golden tan. He looked like a movie star! Just wait till I told Chantal and Katie...

I did my very best to sparkle and to forget about the cement mixer. I giggled, and chatted, and tried to think of witty things to say. I was managing quite well until we got off the bus at Rutger's Park and headed for the boating lake. Keri and Dermot got into one boat, me and Rory in another. The minute we pushed off, the cement mixer went crazy, grinding and pounding. I had to keep my mouth tight shut, with my lips pressed together, not daring to speak or even smile for fear of what might come shooting out. I'd once been violently sick on a cross Channel ferry, when Mum and Dad had taken us to France for a camping holiday. But that had been OK, cos it had got swallowed up by the sea. Imagine being sick in a boating lake! It would all drift there, on the surface; either that, or lie about in clumps at the bottom, for all to see. Just, like, totally *disgusting*.

"Hey," said Rory, as we were finally called in. "Polly's gone green!"

"Yeah, don't worry." Keri flapped a hand. "She gets seasick."

"But there aren't any waves!"

"Don't need waves. She can even get sick just sitting in the bath! Can't you?" She nudged me. I tried to smile, just twitching my lips. "She always got sick, even when we were little. D'you remember?" She nudged me again. I felt my stomach go *blurp!* "Whenever we went on a roundabout, you'd go and bring up. Yuck! Yeeurgh!"

She let her tongue flob out of her mouth, pretending to be me, bringing up.

"Charming," said Dermot.

"What she needs is food." Keri looked at me, rather hard. "Food to *line the stomach*. Yes?"

I nodded, weakly. It is no use trying to fight her. I actually felt a bit better once I was sitting on a bench in the sunshine. The cement mixer subsided, and I nibbled on a KitKat and sipped some lemonade, which Keri said was the best thing for seasickness.

"It's what they used to give sailors...lots of oranges and lemons."

"That was to prevent scurvy," said Dermot.

"*And* seasickness. Drink it all up!"

I glugged it down, thinking that now I would probably need the loo, which is always so embarrassing – though maybe not as embarrassing as being sick.

"That's better," said Keri.

I felt that I would have liked to just go on sitting in the sunshine, but instead we had to go for a walk round the park, which is quite a large one, before catching the bus back into town.

Keri cried, "Pizza, everybody?" As we went into Pizza Express she whispered at me, very fiercely, "You've got to eat. It'll do you good!"

I forced myself to chew a few bits out of the middle of a cheese and tomato pizza, but the cement mixer didn't like it. It began to hurl itself about quite alarmingly, banging and thrashing from one side of my stomach to the other.

"You've gone green again," said Rory. "You OK?"

"Course she is!" Keri sang it out, happily. "Don't encourage her. Polly, *finish your pizza*. Do as you're told!"

"I don't think you should force her," said Rory.

"Trust me," said Keri. "I know what I'm talking about."

She didn't, of course; she has never suffered from cement mixers. I think it is just plain silly to say that these things are all in the mind. They are just as real as a broken leg. I bet she wouldn't say *that* was all in the mind.

"If you were being chased by a Sabretooth tiger," she hissed, as we left the restaurant, "you'd forget about it in an instant!"

I did try, cos I really wanted to impress Rory and show him how bright and amusing I could be, but all I felt like doing was crawling into bed. We went back to Keri's place and shut ourselves away in her sitting room – her *private* sitting room – at the top of the house, and sat around on big squashy cushions on the floor, listening to music. Rory put his arm round me, which should have been *so* romantic, but was totally ruined by my worries about being sick. What if I suddenly threw up all over him? How romantic would *that* be?

"Know what you need?" said Keri. "Brandy! That's the thing for an upset stomach."

Before I could stop her she had gone whizzing downstairs and came whizzing back up again clutching a bottle and a glass.

"Wow! Does your dad know you've got his best Napoleon brandy?" said Dermot.

"It's not his best," said Keri. "I wouldn't take his *best*. This is the stuff Mum keeps in the kitchen. Come on! Open up." She thrust the glass at me. "Swallow!"

"*Ugh.*" I reared away, in horror. "That is foul!"

"Yes, but it's nice when it goes down," said Keri. "All warm and soothing... Take another sip."

She hung over me until I had emptied the whole glass. She was right about it being warm, I felt like I had a furnace roaring inside me. But it was quite soothing; at any rate, it stopped the cement mixer. Maybe, after all, Keri *did* know best. For the next few minutes I burbled and prattled and thought of quite a few witty things to say. Well, they seemed witty to me, and they made everyone laugh.

Rory pulled me close to him and a little tingle ran through me. Definitely a tingle! Snaking round my body, from my fingers to my toes. This was it! What I'd been waiting for. I was normal! The same as everyone else! It had to be some kind of chemistry thing. If the chemistry didn't work, you didn't get the tingle. Like with me and Rees. If Rees had put his arm round me – well! I'd probably have been embarrassed. I'd have gone all stiff and tense. But with Rory ...

73

I flopped back against him. I say *flopped* because something very weird was happening. All my bones seemed to be dissolving, leaving me like a rag doll. Like a pile of jelly. It wasn't unpleasant. In fact, it was really rather soothing. I heard myself give a long, satisfied sigh, and let my head go *flump* against Rory's shoulder.

Somebody laughed; I'm not sure who. Then Rory's voice said, "Hey, you dork, you've gone and got her drunk!"

Drunk? Me? No way! I struggled to sit up, only to fall back again, defeated.

"Drunk as a skunk!"

I waved a hand, in feeble protest.

"How's she gonna get home?

"Oi! Polly." Keri's bony finger poked at me. "How you getting home? Is your dad coming for you?"

I shook my head. Well, moved it slowly from one side to the other. It was as much as I could manage.

"Had I better call him?"

I tried to say no. No, no, no! The last thing I wanted was Dad coming round. I wasn't supposed to be at Keri's. Oh, don't! Please don't!

But of course she did.

Talk about *disaster.*

Chapter 6

"Honestly! It was so *funny*." Keri made a loud braying noise directly into my ear. Laughing, I assumed. Either that or pretending to be a donkey. "You should have seen yourself... You were absolutely *plastered*!"

Whatever that meant. I frowned, and held the phone at arm's length. It was Sunday morning, and I wasn't feeling strong enough to have my eardrums shattered. I didn't see anything to laugh at, in any case. I'd already had Mum all suspicious, sitting on the side of my bed and demanding to know why I'd come home last night smelling of drink. I'd told her the truth about that; how Keri had practically forced me at gunpoint to swallow a whole glass of brandy.

"She said it would take the pain away, which it did, but now," I wailed, "I've got a massive great headache!"

"You would have," agreed Mum. "Brandy is notorious.

Still, at least you won't be doing it again in a hurry!"

I assured her that I wouldn't. "I won't be doing it again, *ever.*"

"A wise decision!"

I'd hoped, after that, she would go away and leave me to snuggle back under the duvet, but instead she turned at the door and said, "What were you doing round at Keri's anyway? I thought you were supposed to be with Dawn?"

Dawn is Frizz's real name: Dawn Frizzell. Apart from her parents, Mum is practically the only person who ever calls her that.

"You said you were spending the afternoon together."

"We were! We did. But then...then we thought..." What? What had we thought? My brain lumbered, sluggishly, trying to dredge up some kind of believable explanation. "We thought we'd go and see Keri!"

"Oh. Well! In future I wish you'd call and let me know. Was Dawn still there when your dad arrived?"

"No," I said. "She'd already gone. She had to leave early."

"That's a pity, she might have kept an eye on you. She's growing into a very sensible young woman."

Was Mum implying that I was growing into a very *stupid* young woman? Cos it always used to be me that was sensible (sort of) and Frizz that had to have an eye kept on her. I wasn't sure I liked this!

And I didn't like Keri shrieking and hooting in my ear, either.

"I don't see what was so funny," I said.

"You! Flopping about all over Rory. He called just now, to find out how you were."

"He did?" I perked up at that. "What did you tell him?"

"Told him you were OK, you just had the curse."

"*What?*" I recoiled, in horror.

"It's always best to be honest about these things," said Keri. "Otherwise he'd have thought you were some raging alcoholic. Either that, or a silly little baby who couldn't even take a sip of brandy without getting roaring drunk. You wouldn't want him to think *that*. Would you?"

I sat, dumb and cross-legged on the bed, covered in crimson shame.

"Well?" said Keri. "*Would* you?"

I came feebly back to life. "I wasn't roaring drunk," I said. "I hardly made a sound!"

"No, you couldn't... You'd completely gone. But you were all over Rory!"

Omigod. This was getting worse and worse. Keri really was the pits. How could she do this to me?

"Just a pity you weren't able to enjoy it!" She chortled, happily. "He did, though. So you see I was *right* to give you brandy, cos if I hadn't you'd have been all prim and boring."

"I wouldn't have been prim!"

"Yes, you would. You know you would. You already were being."

"That's cos I felt sick!"

"And then you drank the brandy and you felt better. So there you are!"

I scrunched my face up into a scowl. "I shouldn't have come. I told you I shouldn't, but you had to go and make me."

"Aw, gee, shucks," said Keri. "I'm real sorry!"

"No, you're not," I said. "You're gloating."

"Why should I be gloating? I'm just glad things worked out."

Worked out? Keri was completely insane.

"I don't see what the problem is," she said. "You're OK now, aren't you?"

Crossly I told her that I was not OK. "I've got people kicking footballs inside my head!"

"Oh, that'll wear off. Just go and take some paracetamol."

"That's what you said yesterday," I reminded her, "and look where it got me!"

"Got you in with Rory, didn't it? I think he's quite gone on you. And you must admit," said Keri, "he's pretty dishy."

Dishy is one of her expressions. She has a whole load of them. Nuts, bonkers, shucks...*dishy.*

78

"Is he or is he not?" she said.

I thought, yes he was, he was *seriously* dishy, and now he wouldn't ever want to see me again. How could Keri have done such a thing? Telling him I had the curse! You just didn't go talking to boys about things like that.

"Well, you don't," I said to Frizz, when I rang her later. "You just *don't*, do you?"

"Well, n-no...I s'ppose not," agreed Frizz, though she didn't sound all that convinced.

"How would you like it if you'd just met this totally gorgeous guy and some idiot went and told him *oh, don't worry, she's just got the curse*?"

"Mm, yes, I see what you mean." I pictured Frizz slowly nodding at the other end of the phone. "Course, I'd tell Darren, but that's different."

I thought yes, Darren wasn't totally gorgeous.

"And I guess you'd tell Rees?"

"You must be joking!"

"You wouldn't even tell Rees? Why wouldn't you tell Rees?"

"Don't see why I should."

"But if you weren't feeling well...it's nothing to be ashamed of."

I just could hardly believe this was Frizz speaking. She used to be so shy and awkward!

"Anyway," she said, "are you telling me this boy was gorgeous?"

"To die for. And now he won't ever want to see me again!"

"Would you want to see him again?"

I would have done – once. Not now. How could I see him again *now*? I'd be far too embarrassed! But I somehow sensed there was no point trying to explain to Frizz.

"I mean, did you actually *like* him?" she said.

"Yes!"

"Or did you just like the way he looks?"

"I said, I liked him!"

"Why did you like him? What did you like about him?"

I drew myself up, very stiff and straight. "Pardon me, but this is not an interrogation," I said.

"I was only asking," said Frizz.

"I don't *know* why I liked him. I just did! And now it's all gone and been ruined, thanks to Keri and her great clattering mouth."

"Except if it wasn't for Keri you wouldn't have met him in the first place."

Frizz really was being *very* annoying. There had once been a time I could always count on her to support me and show sympathy.

"So what are you going to do?" she said.

What could I do? It wasn't up to me.

"What about Rees?"

I didn't want to talk about Rees. I didn't fancy being lectured again.

"Look," I said, "I've got to go. Speak later!"

"OK," said Frizz. "Let me know what happens."

What immediately happened was that Craig pounced on me as I left my room. It was almost like he'd been lying in wait.

"*I* smelt your breath when Dad brought you home last night!"

I regarded him, haughtily. "Excuse me," I said. "Do you mind? You're in the way."

He stepped to one side. "Want a hand?"

Irritably I said, "What for?"

"Can't be too careful with a hangover... Best keep hold of the banisters, don't want to fall down!"

I said, "I am not going to fall down and I do not have a hangover." Even as I said it, footballs thudded round my head. I shoved past. "Why should I have a hangover?"

"Cos you were drunk!"

"Was not!"

"Drunk, drunk! Drunk as a skunk... Wait till Rees gets to hear! All that grief you gave him, then you come home plastered!"

I swung round sharply, and had to grab at the banister rail to keep my balance. "Don't you *dare* tell Rees. If you tell Rees, I swear I'll never forgive you!"

"Think I care?"

"Craig, *please*," I said. "*Please* don't tell him! It was all Keri's fault."

Craig said, "She's a bad influence, she is."

"Who says so?"

"Mum. She says you're too easily impressed by her. But it's all right, you don't have to worry...I don't go round tittle-tattling. I leave that sort of thing to you!"

Normally I'd have hotly denied that I tittle-tattled, but I was just so thankful he wasn't going to tell Rees that for once I let him get away with it. Not only that, men with road drills had now joined the footballers inside my head, and my stomach was plunging and rolling.

"It's your turn to take Bundle out!" yelled Craig, as I reached the bottom of the stairs.

I didn't mind taking Bundle out. If he would just behave himself and let me have a nice gentle stroll...

He did! He can be such a good boy when he wants to. As we were wandering round the park, my phone rang. It was a text message from Rees, saying, *How about next Saturday? Charity dog show Rainbow Pk?* I sank down on to a bench, wondering what to do. Obviously Rory wasn't going to want to see me again; not after yesterday. And a dog show would be fun. I might even be able to enter Bundle for something! I was about to send Rees a text saying that Saturday was OK when the phone rang again. This time it was Keri. What could she want? We'd only spoken a short while ago.

"Hey, Pol! Guess what?" she said. "Dermot just called. He wants to know if we'd like to visit some place called

Hadleigh House next Saturday. You on?"

I blinked. Hadleigh House? That was where Rees had wanted to take me.

"It's boring as hell," said Keri, "but we can get in for free. It's Dermot's uncle's place. They've got old cars there, or something. But next Saturday they're having this fete? Stalls, and stuff? And there's this huge park, with a lake, and deer, and everything. So, you know, it could be OK... Wanna come?"

I hesitated.

"Rory'd like you to!"

I said, *"Honestly?"*

"Honestly!"

I still hesitated. I am never quite sure how much I can rely on Keri. She is one of those people who will say anything to persuade you. I don't mean she tells outright whopping lies, she just tends to get a bit carried away.

"Why would Rory want to see me again?" I said.

"Cos he thinks you're funny! And cute."

That was what she'd said about Dermot: *he* was supposed to think I was cute. Maybe I was! Could I be? *Seriously?* I know I am not beautiful, but one of my grans always says I have a sweet little face. And once when I was going on about being too plump, Dad told me that I wasn't plump, I was cuddly. "Which is far more attractive than a matchstick!" he'd said.

Mum had added that I must learn to value myself a bit

more. "Don't always be putting yourself down."

"OK." I sprang to my feet and called Bundle. The footballers and the pneumatic drills seemed miraculously to have gone. "What time," I said, "and where?"

I texted Rees to apologise and say that unfortunately I couldn't make next weekend. I did feel a bit bad about it, but it wasn't like I'd said I'd see him and then changed my mind. If I'd said I'd see him, then I would have seen him. I wouldn't have let him down; I am not *totally* without principles.

All the same, it did rather niggle at me. I had this irritating voice somewhere inside my head which kept bleating and nagging. But then there was another voice, bolder and more defiant, which kept reminding me that *nothing venture, nothing gain.* You have to take chances if you want to get anywhere in life. On the other hand, I knew for sure I couldn't lie to Mum again.

"Hadleigh House?" said Mum, when I told her. "How are you getting there? How are you getting back?"

I said that Keri's dad was dropping us off, and Dermot's dad was taking us back.

"Back where? To Keri's? I think after yesterday I'd really rather you came straight home."

I said, "*Mu-u-m!*"

"Look, I'm sorry," said Mum, "but I'm not sure how much I like you hanging out with Keri, these days."

"Mum, it'll be all right," I said. "I'm not a *child*."

"You are to me," said Mum. But in the end she agreed I could call home for a lift later in the evening. "Just not *too* late. OK?"

I said OK. And then: "There is just one thing... Does Craig have to know where I'm going?"

"Why on earth shouldn't he?" said Mum.

"Well, cos Rees asked me to go with him, last Saturday, only I couldn't cos of having promised Frizz, and he might be sort of... I dunno! Hurt, or something."

"You mean, if he found out you'd gone with Keri?"

"Yes." I nodded, eagerly. That was it, exactly!

"And you're scared Craig might tell him?"

"Yes."

"Hm." Mum gazed at me through narrowed eyes. "Polly, I don't know what you're playing at," she said, "but it doesn't sound to me as if you're being quite fair with Rees. If you want my opinion, I'd say you ought to go away and think about it."

Well, huh! If that was Mum's opinion I certainly *didn't* want it, thank you very much. I was only trying to spare Rees's feelings! Wouldn't you think she'd appreciate that? Frizz, too. Why did they have to be so...*picky*?

"It just strikes me as odd," said Mum, "that you'd go somewhere with Keri and her boyfriend and not invite Rees to go with you."

She didn't know about Rory. For some reason, I hadn't told her.

"Still, it's your business. I can't lay down the rules for your social life. I only hope you're not doing something you're going to be ashamed of."

There are times I find it a real comfort to discuss things with Mum. Other times, I wish I'd never opened my mouth. This was one of *those* times.

"As for Craig," said Mum, "if he asks you where you're going, I don't expect you to lie to him!"

Chapter 7

I should have known it would all go wrong. I'd been cross with Mum when she'd said about me being ashamed. *I only hope you're not doing something you're going to be ashamed of.*

The reason I'd been cross was that I already *was* ashamed; I just didn't want to admit it. But deep inside me, I knew that I was treating Rees badly. You can't enjoy yourself when you are tortured by feelings of guilt.

The minute we arrived at Hadleigh House I started thinking how Rees had been here last week with his mum and dad: how I could have been here with them. How Rees had so much *wanted* me to be with them. He'd wanted us to have a shared experience. And now I was having it with Keri, instead. And Dermot and Rory, of course. But Dermot had seen it all before, cos of it being his uncle's place, and Rory didn't seem particularly interested. Not even in the old cars, which I thought all boys were fascinated by. As a matter of fact I would have quite liked to look at the cars, just to have something to show off about to Rees.

Not that I would tell him I'd been to Hadleigh, but like if he should pick up an old car magazine in WH Smith, which he sometimes did, I'd be able to point at one and say, "That's a—" something or other. And he would be dead impressed! If we were ever *in* WH Smith again. Together: as a couple. If Rees still wanted us to be. If I still wanted us to be. Which I was beginning to think maybe I did, cos what was I doing here with Keri and her posh friends? I didn't feel comfortable, I obviously didn't fit in. And nobody bothered asking me if *I* would like to go and look at the cars, they just took it for granted that I wouldn't. Keri said, "*Bo-ring!*" and headed off in the direction of the fete.

Fetes are always fun, pretty much whoever you are with, and for a while I managed to forget about Rees. After all, there hadn't been a fete when he was here, so I didn't have to keep thinking, "Last Saturday Rees would have been having a lucky dip," or, "Rees would have been hurling balls at coconuts."

Rory won a teddy bear, which I would have loved, but he said he was taking it back for his little sister. I couldn't help thinking that if Rees had won a teddy bear he would have won it for *me*; but then Rees doesn't have a little sister, so I knew that really I wasn't being fair. I suppose what it was, as well as feeling guilty, I was beginning to feel a bit disgruntled at the way the other three just did their own thing without ever bothering to ask me what I would like to do. For instance, there was a stall selling second-hand books that I could happily have lingered over, but Keri turned her nose up, saying that books were boring.

"We have enough books at school. Come on! Let's go explore the grounds."

If I hadn't, reluctantly, torn myself away, they would just have gone off without me. I suppose I could have stayed, except I didn't know where they were headed. They seemed to be making for the park, which was like *enormous*. I didn't want to get lost!

There were deer in the park. Some of them came ambling up almost within touching distance, but you weren't allowed to feed them, which I thought was a pity.

"They get greedy," said Dermot. "And then they get mean and bite you. My uncle doesn't want people suing him."

"I never heard of anyone being bitten by a deer," I said.

"Well, look, there's notices," said Keri. "And since they're Dermot's uncle's deer, and this is his park, and we got in for free, I'd think the least we could do is stick to the rules."

"I am," I said. "I was just *saying*. Ooh, look, there's

someone with a dog! If I'd known you could bring dogs, I'd have brought Bundle. He'd love all this!"

"Just as well you didn't know, then," said Keri. "Dogs are nothing but a nuisance. We didn't come here to walk dogs!" And then she glanced rather slyly at Dermot and said, "We didn't come here to *walk*."

I was confused: we *were* walking! "So what did we come here for?"

Keri laughed, and Dermot winked. Rory took my hand and swung it. I waited for a tingle, but it didn't happen. I just felt vaguely uncomfortable and couldn't think why.

"This'll do," said Keri, after we'd walked for a bit. "This looks like a nice spot."

She flung herself to the ground. Dermot flung himself after her. Cautiously, I sat down on a clump of tufty grass. Rory sat down next to me. I waited for someone to say something, start a bit of conversation, but nobody did, and I couldn't think of anything. I noticed that Keri and Dermot had gone into some kind of clinch, like they were glued together. A bit embarrassing, really. I am always embarrassed when I see people doing things like that in public. Like once, I went to the cinema with Mum and a couple in front of us were slurping all over each other, and it made me go bright red even in the darkness. Mum said it was bad manners, and I agreed with her.

"Hey! Pol." Rory had his arm round me and was pulling me close to him. I immediately felt myself resisting. What Keri would call *being prim*. "What's the matter?" He tilted my head towards him. His mouth moved in. All flaring and gobbling, like a goldfish. He was going to kiss me! I could see his tongue. Omigod! I didn't want his tongue in my mouth!

"Don't!" I pulled away, sharply, and sat up. "Please!"

"Don't what?" Keri turned, impatiently, to look at me. "For heaven's sake! What is your *problem*?"

My problem was that I shouldn't have come.

I shook my head. "I—"

"What?"

They were all looking at me, now. Keri still impatient, Rory sort of...well! Not best pleased. Dermot lying back, grinning. I was glad *he* found it amusing.

"What is it?" said Keri.

"I...I've forgotten my epi-pen!"

"God," said Keri, "you are such a pain!"

"I know." I hung my head, humbly.

"What's an epi-pen?"

"It's this needle thing she has to stick in herself if she gets stung. Otherwise she goes into shock and *dies*."

"Wow." Rory regarded me with a sort of macabre interest.

"She's looked death in the face," said Keri. And then she turned and screeched at me, "*How could you forget it?*"

I hunched an apologetic shoulder. "Came out in

a rush. I'm really sorry!"

"So what do we do now?" said Dermot.

"*I* don't know. Take her home, I suppose."

Dermot's auntie drove me back. The others didn't come with us; I had the feeling they were just glad to be rid of me. I could understand it, cos I knew I'd been a nuisance and upset all their plans, and now Rory would be like the odd man out and have no one to slurp over. But I just hadn't wanted him slurping over me!

Mum was surprised when I turned up at home in the middle of the afternoon.

"What happened?" she said.

I'd had time to think about this in the car. "I got bored," I said. "Just wandering round doing nothing."

I wasn't telling Mum that I'd forgotten my epi-pen cos a) she'd get in a fret and start telling me how I must never, ever do that again and b) it wasn't even true. It was just something I'd thought up on the spur of the moment, to stop Keri accusing me of being prim. I didn't need Mum reminding me that I had to be careful. It had really scared me, getting stung by a wasp and not being able to breathe. If it hadn't been for Rees dialling 999, I could have died. *And* he'd tried giving me the kiss of life! Not everyone would do that.

I wondered if Rory would have done it, and thought he almost certainly wouldn't. All *he* wanted to do was slurp. Rees didn't slurp. Me and Rees could go for a walk and sit on the grass and just talk, like civilised human beings. The most we ever did was hold hands. It was true I'd sometimes wondered if perhaps we ought to do more, but really, to be honest, I was happy just holding hands. Did that mean Keri was right? Was I really prim?

It was a horrible thought, cos who wants to be prim? I wished there was someone I could talk to about it. I couldn't talk to Mum, cos it would mean telling her about Rory and confessing how unfair I'd been to Rees. Keri was obviously out of the question, and I couldn't even talk to Frizz. She'd already had a go at me. She'd tell me I'd brought it on myself.

"No more than you deserved!"

I knew she'd be right, but I couldn't stand the thought of being lectured again. So who else was there? There was Chloe; she would be sympathetic. Or would she? She'd once told me I was lucky to have a boyfriend. She might not understand how desperately I had yearned for a bit of glamour and romance. I wasn't sure I could understand it myself any more. Perhaps it wouldn't be very diplomatic to moan at Chloe. But I had to confide in someone!

Lily. What about Lily? Yes! I snatched up my phone and dialled her number. When Lily had been in the throes of her heartbreak over Joel, who was the person she had unloaded on? Me! Lily wasn't what you'd call an expert on boys, but at least she wouldn't be censorious. It's one of the best things about Lily, she never *judges* people.

As soon as she answered the phone, I cried, "Lily, I need to talk!"

"Ooh, exciting," said Lily. "What about?"

"Things," I said. "*Boys.*"

"Ooh, even more exciting! On the phone or shall we meet?"

We agreed to meet in half an hour on the top floor of the shopping centre, where they have fountains, and trees in tubs, and little paved areas where you can just sit around. It is such a comfort to have friends who will drop everything at a moment's notice in your hour of need. I said this to Lily and she said, "Well, it's not like I had anything much else to do. And this is exciting!"

"Not really," I said, sounding rather glum.

"So tell, tell!"

So I told, right from the beginning. All about the party, and Dermot thinking I was cute, and me pretending to Rees that I was going off with Frizz, and then telling him I couldn't see him this weekend and letting Keri talk me into another date with Rory, and how it had all gone pear-shaped.

"All because I'm too prim and proper! Least, that's what Keri says."

"What happened?" breathed Lily.

"Well, we went to this Hadleigh House place, and Keri wanted to wander about in the park, and we all sat down

94

and she and Dermot immediately started snogging, and Rory just sort of…*grabbed* me."

"Grabbed you!"

"Yes."

"Then what happened?"

"He tried to kiss me. I don't even know him!" I wailed.

"You mean you didn't fancy him?"

"No! Well – not that much. I mean…he's OK. To look at. You *could* fancy him. I sort of did, to begin with. I just didn't want to snog with him!"

"And there's no reason you should have," said Lily, soothingly.

"You really think so?"

"There isn't any law says you have to snog if you don't want to."

"You don't think I was just being prim?"

"I think you were just being choosy," said Lily. "That's your right! Boys can't go round just grabbing at people willy-nilly."

I giggled at that, and Lily did, too. It is such a funny expression! *Willy-nilly.*

"Well, but they can't," said Lily, when we'd stopped giggling. "Some boys just behave *so* badly." And then she said, "What was he actually like? Apart from wanting to snog. I mean…what made you go out with him in the first place?"

I said that it was Keri. "She kind of twisted my arm.

I said why didn't she ask you, b—"

"Why didn't she?" said Lily.

"She said she did."

"Oh," said Lily, "she is such a liar!"

"You mean, she *didn't*?"

"No, she swear words didn't! Pardon my French," said Lily.

So Frizz was right all along, I thought. Keri had only asked me because she didn't want to run the risk of Lily enticing Dermot away from her.

"It's a pity she didn't," I said, rather bitterly.

"Well, I think it is, too," said Lily. "Considering she's my best friend, *supposed* to be."

"Would you have gone?"

"I might have."

"What about Joel?"

"Joel isn't my *boy*friend." Lily said it earnestly. "I love him to bits and I absolutely adore dancing with him, but I know in my heart of hearts he's not going to stop being gay just cos of me."

"You could always ring Keri and tell her you're free," I said.

"Not sure I'd want to, now," said Lily. "Not now I've heard your story."

"But you might *like* snogging with the creep."

"Yes, and I might not! What are you going to do about Rees?"

"Dunno." I snapped off a bit of twig from a nearby tree. "Apologise, I s'ppose."

"You going to tell him you went out with Keri?"

"No!" I shook my head, violently.

"So what are you going to apologise for?"

"Just…I don't know!" I flung the twig away from me. I hadn't really thought things out. I knew Rees *deserved* an apology, cos it wasn't just boys that behaved badly. I'd behaved badly, too! But how could I tell him what I'd done? I couldn't! I'd be too ashamed.

"All this dating stuff," said Lily. "It's so complicated, isn't it?"

I sighed. "It is for some of us. Keri doesn't seem to have any problems. Nor does Frizz. Darren's like almost the only boy she's ever been out with."

"Frizz is one of the lucky ones," said Lily. "And Keri – well! She's just Keri. She'll probably end up being married and divorced a zillion times."

"Chance would be a fine thing," I muttered.

"You don't mean that," said Lily. "You're not the sort to go round having multiple relationships. Neither am I, I don't think. Know what I reckon? I reckon you ought to pick up the phone right now and call Rees."

"And say what? I don't know what to say to him!"

"Anything! Doesn't matter. Just so long as you're talking."

"Or I could send him a text," I said.

"Well, you could," agreed Lily. "But that would be cowardly."

Would it? I looked at her, doubtfully.

"You know it would!"

She was right. Rees had been brave enough to ring *me*, after our day out in Brighton when he had drunk too much and thrown up all over everywhere on the train back. The least I could do was be equally brave.

"All right, I'll do it," I said.

"Way to go!" cried Lily.

I made a sudden decision: "I'll do it *right now*!"

Lily nodded, encouragingly. "Before you can change your mind."

It was true, if I waited till I got home I might well have second thoughts. It wasn't going to be easy, talking to Rees.

"You've got to do it," urged Lily.

"Right." I took a deep breath and dialled Rees's number. Lily stood, watching me. I said, "Rees?" Lily nodded, encouragingly. "Rees, it's me!" Like he didn't already know. "I'm really, really, *really* sorry about today! It was just...something I couldn't get out of. You know what it's like! You make these arrangements and then when the time comes you wish you hadn't but you can't think of any excuse. You know?"

"That's OK," said Rees.

Oof! I let out my breath in a big *whoosh.* He

98

understood! He wasn't mad at me. Lily stuck up a thumb then tapped a finger against her watch and pointed at the exit.

"OK?"

I nodded and waved a hand. Lily had proved to be a real, true friend; she had given me the best advice of anyone.

"How about next Saturday?" I said, watching as Lily went walking off towards the escalator, with her back held very straight and her feet turned out, the way dancers always walk. "What I was thinking," I said, "I was thinking maybe you were right about those obedience classes? Maybe I gave up too easily?" I wasn't any keener on them than I'd been before, but Rees had enjoyed them and I felt I owed it to him. "S'ppose we go back and I try again?" I said. "And this time, I promise, I'll make a real effort!"

About the Author

Jean Ure had her first book published while she was still at school and immediately went rushing out into the world declaring that she was AN AUTHOR. But it was another few years before she had her second book published, and during that time she had to work at lots of different jobs to earn money. In the end she went to drama school to train as an actress. While she was there she met her husband and wrote another book. She has now written more than eighty books! She lives in Croydon with her husband and their family of seven rescued dogs and four rescued cats.

Girlfriends

Don't miss any of the other Girlfriends books!
Turn the page for a peek at the first in the series...

978 1 84616 961 8 £4.99

Chapter 1

"Honestly! Just look at that girl," said Keri.

In the middle of the playground, in full view of absolutely everyone, Jessamy Jones was standing on her head. Her legs were in the air, and her skirt had gone *flump!* all over her face.

"Showing off," I said.

"Don't worry," said Lily. "She'll fall over in a minute."

But she didn't. Worse luck! She went on standing there, upside down, surrounded by a group of admirers. All girls from our class. Jessamy Jones is in our class. *Unfortunately*. She is someone we hold in total contempt.

"Lily could do what she's doing," said Frizz.

"Yes, I could," said Lily. "But I wouldn't...not in front of everyone. Specially not in front of *boys.*"

It wasn't the boys' playground, but they can easily see into it from theirs.

"There's a gang of them watching right now," I said.

Lily sucked in her breath.

"Look at those knickers!" said Keri.

We looked. To be perfectly honest, they just seemed like ordinary knickers to me. I mean, she oughtn't to have been showing them, and she is a total grot, and I despise her utterly, but I couldn't actually see anything wrong with her knickers.

"*Pink,*" said Keri.

"Ugh! Groo!" said Lily.

Keri sniffed. "Well, but I ask you!"

So then I knew that pink knickers were naff. Keri is our authority on these things; she is really cool! She can even make school uniform seem like designer clothes. You should see her at weekends! Ten going on twenty, my mum says. If Keri tells us that pink knickers are naff, then we don't wear them. It's as simple as that.

I made a note to take out and lose ALL THE ONES

I had in my drawer at home. From this point on, I wouldn't be seen dead in them!

"Great galloping grandmothers! Now look at it," said Keri.

It was walking on its hands. Quite clever, really. But not more than Lily could have done! Lily just doesn't show off like some people. She is quite modest.

Suddenly, as we sat sourly watching, Frizz burst out with:

"Is pink bad?"

Oh, dear! Poor Frizz. She is so embarrassing at times. Lily giggled. Keri rolled her eyes.

"Get real!" she said.

"Well, but I don't see what's wrong with it," said Frizz. "I've got pink knickers." And she hoicked up her skirt to show us.

I suppose in a way it was quite brave. If I'd been wearing pink knickers I'd have died sooner than let on! But I sometimes seriously feel that Frizz is just a tiny bit young for her age. I guess it comes from having a mum and dad that are ancient. More like a nan and granddad, really. It makes them a bit old-fashioned so they think that at ten years old Frizz is still a young child. Instead of, as we keep reminding her, practically a teenager!

£4.99   978 1 84616 963 2

Despite being at her new school with
the uncool Jessamy James, Polly's making plenty
of new friends and earning herself a whole new
social life. But will new arrangements clash with
the gang of four's weekly Saturday meet-ups?

Will Polly be facing a friendship crisis? Or will the
girlfriends work it out?

What's up with Frizz?

The gang of four are eager to talk about their talents, but Frizz is keeping quiet. Whatever happened to sharing everything and sticking together? Is Polly right in thinking she's just jealous, overshadowed by too much talent?

Or does Frizz have a secret of her own to share that will steal the spotlight?

978 1 84616 964 9

£4.99

The girlfriends are growing up and entering a whole new world, and boys are a major part of it. After their separate summer holidays, Polly is alarmed when her friends start showing an interest in boys, but is even more alarmed when boys start showing an interest in her! Reluctant to grow up, will Polly be left behind? Or will she realise that not all boys are what they seem...?

978 1 40830 301 6

£4.99

The Gang of Four are growing up. It seems to Polly that they spend most of their spare time with their boyfriends, and even when they are together, all they do is talk about boys. Polly's not sure whether boys really *are* her. Wasn't it better when it was just the four girls and they could shop, gossip and not have to worry about boys all the time? Polly wonders whether she'll ever really understand what it's all about...

Girlfriends

Boys Are Back

JEAN URE

978 1 40830 304 7

£4.99

Polly and Rees have split up, but Polly's not sure she wants to be like Keri – who's never seems to stick with the same boy. Perhaps it is time to do new things…and meet new people. But will Polly be brave – and does she really want to leave Rees behind?

Orchard Books are available from all good bookshops, or can be ordered from our website: www.orchardbooks.co.uk, or telephone 01235 827702, or fax 01235 827703.